By

Victoria Chatham

Print ISBN: 9781771455046

Books We Love, Ltd.
Calgary, Alberta
Canada

Copyright 2015 by Victoria Chatham

Cover art by Michelle Lee Copyright 2015

All rights reserved. Without limiting the rights under copyright reserved above, no part of this publication may be reproduced, stored in or introduced into a retrieval system, or transmitted, in any form, or by any means (electronic, mechanical, photocopying, recording, or otherwise) without the prior written permission of both the copyright owner and the publisher of this book.

Dedication
To the cowboys and rodeo performers who answered all my questions with grace and good humor.

Acknowledgements
Thank you to my fantastic critique partners A.M. Westerling and Brenda Sinclair

Chapter One

Trisha Watts closed her eyes, muttering a prayer to the gods of the airways for a safe landing. The plane banked and leveled into its flight path. The change in pressure made her ears pop. Yawning and swallowing in quick succession did little to alleviate the pain. Even being in a coma for eight weeks would be preferable to this unexpected result of her accident. Her stomach lurched and she held herself tightly.

Her last-minute booking secured her a seat towards the plane's tail-end but it didn't matter where she sat, her nerves now jangled from take-off to landing on any flight. The plane approached the runway in what seemed interminable degrees. With barely a bump to indicate when it landed, it touched down and raced along the tarmac. The reverse engines roared, reverberating through her head until she wanted to scream.

Her fellow passengers rushed to deplane but not wanting to be part of the crush, she calmed herself as she unbuckled her seat belt and simply waited her turn. As soon as she had room to move Trisha stood up, stepped into the aisle and reached up to the overhead compartment for her carry-on.

"Let me get that for you."

A man's long-fingered hand brushed past hers.

"Thanks, I can manage." She flashed a glance at the owner of the hand.

"I'm sure you can." His disarming smile showed even white teeth, the result she suspected of healthy living or a very good dentist. "But my momma raised me to always help a lady."

"Then you'd make your momma very proud." Trisha stepped back. Her helper's large frame completely overwhelmed her own five foot seven inches.

Mischief sparked in his smoky-grey eyes. He held the carry-on's handle for a moment more as if aware his assistance irritated her. "This looks pretty beat up. You travel a lot?"

"Only when I have to." Given a choice she preferred a cozy room and a good book to a packed airplane.

He grunted a little as he lifted the carry-on from the compartment. "You carrying the kitchen sink in here?"

"It's my camera kit."

"Must be some camera."

"I'm a photo-journalist and that case contains several pieces of very valuable equipment. Please be careful with it."

She reached for the handle but he continued to hold it. With amusement in his eyes and a teasing smile on his face, he made sure his fingers grazed hers before finally relinquishing his grip. His touch raised goose bumps on her skin, from pleasure or apprehension she couldn't immediately determine.

"Thank you." She turned on her heel to join the shuffling line of passengers.

"You're welcome, ma'am."

The hot breath of his whisper lingered on her neck. Intuition told her he'd intended it to. She bit back a hasty comment, not wanting to give him the satisfaction of knowing he'd rattled her composure. Despite his attempt to help her, she thought his momma may not have approved of his teasing.

At the exit she thanked the cabin staff flanking the doorway and sighed with relief as she stepped onto the gangway. Relief fled when her would-be helper quickly caught up with her.

"Goin' my way?" he asked as he settled a wide-brimmed cowboy hat on his head.

Trisha shook her head. Heaven help him if that was his only pick-up line.

Striding along the gangway to get ahead of him, she stopped when he overtook her. He winked at her but before she could vent her frustration with him, he walked away. People who were coming up behind her grumbled that she was in their way and she started forward again. Now trailing the large figure by several yards she kept her distance, hoping he'd accepted that she wasn't interested in him or his banter.

Annoyed with herself for not being able to take her eyes off his broad shoulders and slim hips, she continued to lag behind. His plaid shirt and denim jeans looked clean and fresh after the long flight, while her clothes were crumpled and creased. Even his boots, though worn at the heel, were clean. He looked every inch a cowboy and so very appealing, but none knew better than she how deceiving looks could be.

Trisha tried not to think about him but then he passed her while she waited at the luggage carousel. This time he didn't offer to help.

"Welcome to Calgary, ma'am. Hope you enjoy your stay in our city." He tipped his hat to her and sauntered off.

"Hope there's a sunset for you to ride into, cowboy," she muttered as she grabbed her suitcase and made her own way out into the concourse.

Momentarily disoriented Trisha stopped to get her bearings. The crowd flowed around her and moved on. She watched families greet each other with open arms. Cab drivers held name cards and waited patiently for their fares. Friends greeted each other with a handshake or a slap on the back, but of her friend Samantha Monroe, who had promised to not be late, there was no sign.

Trisha sighed. She'd learnt soon after they'd first met that 'on time' and 'Samantha' could not be mentioned in the same breath. She'd be late for her own funeral and how she managed to run a successful modeling agency was beyond Trisha's comprehension. She reached into her canvas shoulder bag for her cell phone but looked up when someone called her name.

A petite figure sporting spiky white-blonde short hair rushed towards her. Elbows flying, ducking and dodging bodies much bigger than her own, she resembled a demented pixie.

"Hi, you must be Trisha Watts, I'm Dee." She grabbed the baggage cart and held up a battered photo of Trisha as if it was proof she'd met the right person. "Samantha's been held up, she's trying to get a new model under contract but the girl definitely has her own ideas. Has some outrageous demands and Samantha's almost tearing her hair out over it. She said to take you straight to her apartment and she'll join you as soon as the ink is dry. Come on, this way."

Dee's rapid-fire chatter continued non-stop as she led the way to the waiting car. Trisha could barely get a word in edgewise and gave up in disgust. How like Samantha to have hired a doppelganger.

Dee kept up her verbal onslaught as they drove towards Calgary's downtown core. To Trisha, one city was much like another. Too many people, too much traffic and, more often than not, too little time for her to explore them anyway. In spite of her doubts Trisha found the compact city skyline far more appealing than she'd expected it to be. An ultramodern angular building bristling with steel and glass caught her attention.

"What's that place?" she asked.

"Our new science centre." Dee slid the car easily into the flow of traffic heading into the city. "That's the zoo on the left and the Bow River and we'll soon take a short cut through Chinatown. Do you like Chinese food?"

"Yes, I do. I also like Greek, Italian and Indian food too, but not necessarily in that order." Trisha didn't add her opinion that those foods tasted best when eaten in their countries of origin.

"Calgary's really cosmopolitan," Dee continued. "You'll find all that and more here. But through Stampede people mostly survive on breakfast fare by day and beer by night. Sometimes we even combine them."

"Beer with breakfast?" Trisha shuddered at the thought. "You are joking?"

"Nope, all the sausages and pancakes you could ever hope for are served up free all over the city throughout the ten days of Stampede."

The thought of living on a combination of breakfast and beer for ten days made Trisha feel slightly nauseous and she breathed a sigh of relief when the car stopped. The engine purred like a happy cat while Dee pressed a remote control device clipped onto the visor. She hadn't yet drawn breath as far as Trisha could tell and the chattering continued as she unloaded the car and led the way to the elevator. Trisha followed, amazed that Samantha's assistant was still talking.

"But you know Samantha. When I told her it wasn't really her business, she fired me. Again. Here we are."

Dee flung open an apartment door. Trisha followed her inside and stopped on the threshold, stunned by the stark white walls and a grey tiled floor that shimmered like quicksilver. Sunlight poured relentlessly through the large, bare windows adding to the impression of light and space.

"Very Samantha." Trisha trailed her hand over the back of a zebra-patterned designer sofa. She doubted it would be comfortable. A huge red velvet cushion propped at one end provided an eye-popping color contrast.

"I know." Dee grinned at Trisha's surprise. "Everyone has the same reaction to it. Samantha has this great interior designer. He so loved this remodel he's featured it in loads of magazines. Your room's down here. Has its own en-suite. Coffee machine's in the kitchen. Or would you prefer tea? It can brew either. Oh, and wine in the fridge. Anything else you'd like?"

Trisha sat down on the end of a queen-sized bed covered in shadow-striped white linens and tried to catch up.

"Coffee, tea, wine. I think I've got it, thank you." How hard could it be?

Dee wiggled her fingers as a goodbye, assured her Samantha should be with her right away, and left.

Trisha didn't even hear the door close. Peace and quiet at last, thank god, just her and her thoughts which, if she let them, pulled her down to a place she did not want to be. She rubbed a hand over her eyes. No point in dwelling on the past.

Right now she had a contract to fulfill photographing rodeo stock and interviewing owners and riders. Where better place to do that, the editor at Equine World magazine suggested, than the Calgary Stampede? Oh, and by the way you don't happen to know anyone who lives there, do you?

Trisha sighed. Oh for the days of all-expenses paid trips. After some consideration she'd contacted Samantha knowing that any request she made, for accommodation or otherwise, would probably carry some caveat.

Of course come and stay with me, Samantha had cooed. You can help me choose pictures of cowboys, hot cowboys at that, for the agency.

Trisha almost smiled at the memory. Having been a photo-journalist for almost a decade, she knew she had all the right credentials to help Samantha pick the most photogenic models. Yet a haze of doubt clouded her mind. She owed Samantha a favor, and a pretty big one at that. Her gut told her there would be more to it but, heck, it should be a breeze. Shouldn't it? Pick a couple of photos for goodness' sake and it was done.

The image of the cowboy on the plane drifted into her mind.

"I so hope you're not one of them," she muttered as she lay back on the bed.

* * *

The sky could not have been bluer or the ...
Trisha's eyes flew open. God, when would that dream stop haunting her? Her chest still felt tight with panic as she pushed herself up against the pillows and looked around. Where was she? Then she remembered. With a sigh of relief she swung her legs off the bed, stood up and stretched the kinks out of her back as Samantha walked into the room.

"What a bitch of a day," she complained in a voice made husky with too many cigarettes and late nights.

"Hello, Samantha. It's good to see you, too." Trisha couldn't keep an edge of sarcasm out of her voice at the brusque greeting.

"Oh, hell." Trisha's sarcasm faded into a grin as Samantha pulled her into a rough hug. "Don't mind me, I'm being crabby. How was your flight?"

"Took off from Heathrow, landed in Calgary. What more can I say?"

Trisha subjected herself to a thorough inspection as Samantha held her at arm's length. "Your hair's different since I last saw you and when did you get so skinny?"

"It's a girl's prerogative to change her hair style and you're a fine one to be calling me skinny," Trisha countered. "What marvel diet are you on these days?"

"We're not talking about me," Samantha said. "You look like you should be in front of the camera, not behind one. Need an agent?"

Trisha's insides flipped at the thought. "No thank you."

"Hmm. Pity."

Trisha didn't miss the speculative gleam in Samantha's eyes and knew questions were being stored in her friend's mental filing cabinet. At some point she would start probing for answers that Trisha would rather not give. Just then her stomach growled, reminding her that she hadn't eaten for several hours. Samantha didn't miss it either.

"Do you want to eat out or in?" she asked.

"Whichever's easiest, but first I'm having a shower."

"Go for it." Samantha sat on the end of the bed. "Everywhere's going to be crazy with the Greatest Outdoor Show on Earth about to start, but it's still early enough to go shopping and get you duded up."

Trisha stuck her head around the bathroom door. "Duded up?"

"Yep, pardner." Samantha tried to hide her amusement behind a serious expression but failed. "From shirts and jeans to boots and a hat, you need everything cowboy. I can't possibly take you out on the town unless you are dressed western. Please don't tell me you're too stuffy for that."

Trisha snorted with unladylike laughter and closed the door.

* * *

Samantha flicked through racks packed with shirts in a variety of styles and colors. She pulled out a black then a purple eyelet shirt for Trisha to try on.

"Here, this purple one will bring out the green in your eyes." She thrust the shirt at Trisha. "It has darts front and back, so should really show off your waist too."

Running a practiced glance over Trisha's slim hips and long legs, she then selected four pairs of jeans.

"Here you are, size ridiculous in a thirty-four inch leg." She added the jeans to the pile of shirts and pushed Trisha into a changing room. "Start trying that lot on. Here's a pair of boots for you and I'll get you a hat."

"A hat? Are you sure I need one?"

Samantha nodded her head firmly, leaving no room for argument. "I'll go and find you a belt with a snazzy buckle too. A girl's got to have bling."

"What's so great about bling," Trisha mumbled to herself as she pulled on a pair of jeans stiff with newness, tucked the shirttail into the waistband and zipped up. She pushed the swinging doors open. "Hey Samantha, what do you think ..."

The squeak from the door hinges covered Trisha's whispered "hell" as her footsteps faltered. Her eyes narrowed as she recognized the customer at the sales counter.

That cowboy again.

She'd judged him to be at least six foot four inches tall and would know that frame anywhere. Stepping back into the changing room, she hoped he hadn't seen her. He'd irritated her this morning with his goofy grin and smart remarks. One half of her mind never wanted to see him again. The other half juggled with whether she should take another look at him or not.

Or not would be the sensible choice.

Or not lost.

Taking a tentative step forward she peered around the changing room door.

A fresh, crisp white shirt did nothing to hide his wide shoulders and broad back. It showed off biceps a body-builder would be proud of. His clean but well-worn blue jeans fit snug on his hips and thighs. He looked down at something the clerk placed on the counter and she glimpsed the straight-cut line of dark brown hair across the back of his neck.

Something the clerk said made him laugh and at the sound of it, unexpected and unwelcome warmth swirled in her belly. What was with that? It was bad enough that she hadn't forgotten his smoky-grey eyes, screened with thick black lashes that shouldn't be allowed on a man.

As she watched him, he straightened up and flexed his shoulders. Her gaze tracked the play of muscles beneath the cotton fabric covering them, setting every nerve in her body aquiver. He turned his head from side to side to stretch his neck and she glimpsed the strong line of his jaw and his firm, square chin. Right then the hope she harbored that he might be some kind of mirage vanished.

Nope, this man was a real life heart attack on legs. Her mouth dried in an instant, puckering as if she'd sucked on a slice of lemon.

Furious with herself for her reaction at seeing him again, she let go of the breath she held. She stumbled back into the changing room and collapsed onto the narrow, slatted seat. Built more for holding clothes than a dead weight with rubber legs, she hoped it would hold her.

This morning she never wanted to see him again. This afternoon he sent her pulse into overdrive. Somewhere between then and now the synapses in her brain must have misfired. That could be the only reason for her ridiculous about turn from a cool, collected professional to behaving like a teenager on her first crush.

She peered out of the changing room once more. The clerk busily wrapped something while the cowboy looked on. Samantha had promised her hot cowboys but this one sizzled like water dropped on hot coals.

Body parts she'd forgotten existed made themselves known to her in an explosive surge. Catching her lower lip between her teeth she bit down hard, wincing at the pain. She would not let this happen; would not let herself be overwhelmed by a complete stranger.

"Hey, you okay in there?"

Samantha's voice jolted her back into the here and now, bringing Trisha to her feet. She pushed her hair out of her eyes and shook the tension from her arms. Lifting her chin a notch she shouldered her way through the slatted swinging doors and twirled around for Samantha's expert opinion.

"Much, much better," Samantha announced as she held out a white hat.

After a moment's hesitation, Trisha settled it on her head and tucked strands of her dark brown hair behind her ears. Samantha adjusted the hat slightly before nodding with satisfaction.

"Now step into those boots."

Trisha stared down at the silver trimmed, tooled black leather boots Samantha had found for her. They were gorgeous. She pulled on the right boot, the supple leather wrapping around her foot like her mother's warm hug.

"Samantha, you're amazing," she exclaimed as she put her left foot into the other boot. "These fit perfectly. How do I look?"

"From where I'm standing, you look pretty damn fine."

Both women looked up at the sound of a deep baritone voice. That such a big a man could move so quietly amazed Trisha.

Samantha read her witless expression in one swift glance and agreed with him, giving Trisha a chance to regain her composure.

Mr. Heart-Attack-on-Legs gave her a smoldering grey-eyed once over and she straightened her spine. How dare he sneak up on her?

"May I?" He reached out and adjusted the collar on her shirt, then wound a wayward strand of hair around his finger before brushing it back off her shoulder.

He scarcely touched her, yet the heat and strength of his fingers seared her skin through the thin fabric. In a whirl of confusion she sensed tenderness in that touch, nothing like the brash casualness she'd experienced from him that morning.

Against her better judgement she tipped her head back so she could see him more clearly from beneath the brim of her hat and then wished she hadn't. She couldn't tear her eyes away from his and the smart reply her mind produced got lost in transit to her lips.

He aimed a slow, mind-blowing sexy smile directly at her. Her heart swelled and bumped painfully against her ribs. He tipped his hat and winked at her as he left the store.

Trisha watched him go, every breath in her body trailing after him and leaving her breathless.

Samantha, a tiny smirk of amusement twisting her lips, eyed Trisha with sly humor.

"I think that you," she announced, "are definitely in trouble."

Chapter Two

Cameron Carter cursed under his breath for being an idiot as he strode down the mall.

One look at his grim expression sent people scattering out of his way rather than risk being plowed under. When he reached the entrance door he pushed it open, strode across the sidewalk and halted on the curb.

The evening air, still heavy with the heat of the day and clogged with dust and vehicle fumes, almost choked him when he took a deep breath.

What on earth had possessed him to touch the woman? He cursed himself every which way. She could've screamed blue bloody murder. Instead, she'd looked at him all wide eyed and not a clue what to do. He hooked his thumbs into the belt loops on his jeans as if to anchor himself and shook his head in disbelief at his own actions.

He took three long steps along the sidewalk. The sensation of the light fabric of her shirt and the outline of her collar bone still remained on his fingertips. That prominent collar bone bothered him. She wasn't simply slim, she was thin. Spinning on his heel he strode back to his starting point. How dumb a conclusion was that? He didn't know anything about her. She could be tough as nails, like some of the barrel racers he met up with on the rodeo circuit. No meat on them but fit and wiry and strong as all get out.

That she was all woman he had no doubt. Her shirt did nothing to hide the swell of her small breasts, nor the slim waist above a flat stomach and taut hips. And as for those long denim-covered legs? Man, she could wrap them around him anytime.

What the hell happened back there? He'd been talking to the store manager about the silver belt buckle he'd ordered and then he heard her.

How was that even possible? The crazy buzz of people in the mall drifted through the store's open doors adding to the existing hum of conversation inside. The steady cadence of her English accent, clear and easy to listen to, rose above it all and he'd turned in her direction.

She and another woman were checking out new duds and before he could stop himself he'd stepped up and offered his opinion.

The hand he rubbed over his face did nothing to erase the image of her bright, emerald green eyes. Damn, but he was a sucker for any shade of green eyes. Always had been, likely always would be. But that wasn't why he'd wanted to touch her. There was something else. Something bone-deep that drew him to her, as if his body knew something his brain didn't. Whatever it was he couldn't quite figure it out and probably shouldn't even try.

Heading out into the crowded parking lot, Cameron located his truck, unlocked it and stepped back to avoid the blast of built-up heat as he opened the door. He fitted his key into the ignition and started the engine but waited a moment for the AC to kick in and cool the cab down. If he hadn't promised to meet his buddy for a beer, he'd have hit the highway and headed straight back to his ranch.

His phone blasted its barking-dog ring-tone and Cameron grabbed it out of his pocket. He recognized Greg Tooley's number in the display panel and took the call.

"I'm just leaving the mall, bud. Stay put, I'll be with you as soon as I can."

A muscle twitched in his jaw as he grimaced in frustration at the sight of three lanes of gridlock on Macleod Trail. With Stampede starting in two days, there was no possible way to avoid the traffic. It took him nearly thirty minutes to get from the mall lot and find another parking spot at the bar where he'd arranged to meet Greg.

A hostess flashed him a bright smile as he entered the pub's cool interior, but he'd already spotted Greg and wove his way between the tables to join him.

"What's up?" He dropped his truck keys on the table top and sat down.

Greg tilted his bottle of beer and inspected the label as if he'd never seen that particular brew before. A waitress appeared and Cameron ordered one of the same.

"I've done something real stupid." Greg said.

"Tell me something new." Cameron remembered his own stupidity back at the store and added under his breath, "We're both guilty of that."

The waitress returned with a frosty bottle, placed a small napkin on the table and set the bottle on it. Cameron nodded his thanks.

"Damn it, this is serious." Greg raked his fingers through his hair, leaving it ruffled and untidy. "You know the state I'm in with my place?"

"You told me the bank wouldn't allow you an extension." Cameron waited patiently for whatever would come next.

Greg nodded slowly. "Now I have to come up with a lot of bucks fast to avoid losing everything."

"Any idea how you're going to do that?"

Greg took another sip of his beer and without a word slid a creased business card across the table.

Cameron picked it up and read, 'Samantha Monroe Modeling Agency'. For a moment he said nothing. Then he grinned and chuckled with amusement.

"You're right." He lifted his bottle and tipped it in salute to Greg. "That is stupid."

"This Monroe woman said I could earn a lot of money modeling." Cameron couldn't fail to see the misery in Greg's clear blue eyes. "When she told me what I could expect in fees,

I near fell off my chair. But there's a snag. A big one."

Now curious, Cameron sat back in his chair and watched Greg through narrowed eyes while he waited for an answer.

"And that is?" he prompted when it seemed that Greg had lost his tongue.

Greg took a deep breath and swallowed hard, the Adam's apple in his throat bobbing nervously. "My best shot gets entered in a competition for some kind of book cover deal."

"What kind of books?" Cameron asked cautiously.

Greg hung his head. "Western romance novels."

Cameron choked back his laughter. "What does your wife think of all this?"

"I haven't told Donna," Greg admitted. "She'll kill me when she finds out."

"Aw, damn." Cameron plunked his bottle down. "I get it now."

"What the hell am I supposed to do?" Greg pleaded as he leaned across the table.

"Well, bud, as I remember it you've always, for whatever knuckle-headed reason, gone your own way regardless of what Donna wants. She's got to love you one helluva lot to put up with you, you jerk." Cameron heard the tinge of envy in his voice as he stared Greg down. "I'm guessing what's really eating you up right now is the fact you know she deserves better."

Greg stared back with his jaw stubbornly clenched, but then his glance shifted. "Oh, hell."

"What?" Cameron straightened up, alarmed at Greg's sudden and obvious dismay.

"Samantha Monroe just walked in." Greg grabbed his hat off the seat beside him, settled it firmly on his head and pulled the brim down over his eyes.

Cameron looked up, surprised to see the girl and her friend from the store. It didn't take two guesses for him to decide which was which. The woman asking the hostess for a booth had to be Samantha Monroe. The girl with her looked uncomfortable, as if not sure of herself in her new clothes. She hooked her dark brown hair behind her ears and adjusted her hat. The fog in his brain suddenly cleared. That air she had about her, the one he hadn't been able to immediately identify? He saw it now as he recognized an expression of vulnerability in her green eyes. It made him want to scoop her into his arms and hold her tight. Sensations he hadn't contemplated in a long time hit him hard and he exhaled slowly.

"Evening, Greg," Samantha said as she passed their table.

"Ma'am." Greg tipped his hat and let out a breath.

Cameron tore his glance from the slim figure setting his whole body on red alert and surveyed her companion. "That woman's the Samantha Monroe who hired you to model?"

"No, that's a shark in woman's clothing who hired me to model," Greg muttered under his breath. "Didn't realize it until after I signed the dotted line on her damn contract. How the hell do I get out of this fix?"

"Don't know, but I guess if you want that cash you'll just have to suck it up. You'll figure it out," Cameron said with a chuckle. "Who's the girl with her? She sounds like she may be English."

"English?" Greg peered over his shoulder. "Jeez, that must be the gal from London who's judging the competition entries. Hell, I'm outta here."

He downed the rest of his beer in one long swallow, threw a ten-dollar bill on the table and left.

Cameron picked up the bill and idly smoothed it out while he thought about the step Greg was about to take. Even though it was to save their home, Donna would likely ring a peel over his head when she found out about it. They reminded him of his parents. Always giving and taking, they shared the good as well as the bad. He'd never experienced that kind of relationship. Never even come close to it. He'd for sure enjoyed the girls who came in and out of his life and thought he treated them well. At least none had ever complained about his lovemaking. Heck, when was the last time that had even happened?

Building a home and a business that no one could take away from him took priority over everything else. Marriage, when it crossed his mind, was always at some time in the future. He glanced briefly towards the girl who'd stirred those thoughts in him but when he stood to leave, Samantha Monroe smiled at him.

Since she'd caught his eye, he could hardly ignore her. He gave her a brief smile and she beckoned him over to their booth. When he approached he saw the predatory gleam in her dark, almond-shaped eyes and when she smiled Cameron immediately saw why Greg likened her to a shark.

"Mr ...?" She held out her hand.

"Carter, Ma'am. Cameron Carter," he said as he took it and gave it a brief shake.

"Why don't you join us?"

Cameron hesitated. He couldn't deny that finding out more about the English girl might be extremely interesting, but what did Samantha Monroe want with him?

"Oh, come on Mr. Carter." Samantha patted the seat beside her. "I'm not going to bite and besides, I'm getting a crick in my neck looking up at you. What do you boys put in your pancakes to make you grow so tall?"

Samantha he could take or leave, and would definitely like to leave, but his interest in the girl with her might be somewhat satisfied if he stayed. He ignored the question with a shrug and sat down.

"What can I do for you Ms. Monroe?"

"Oh, don't be silly." She patted his arm. "It's Samantha. And I'm wondering if you might know of someone who could help my friend, Trisha, here. You see," she moved in a little closer and whispered in his ear, "she used to ride but hasn't been on a horse in ages."

Cameron pictured Trisha's jean-clad rear slapping a saddle and a smile spread slowly across his face. "Can you ride?"

Trisha looked at him as if she wished he were elsewhere. "I've ridden a camel, a donkey and an elephant."

Her green eyes held him in a steady stare as she evaded his question.

"I meant can you ride a horse?"

Her mouth tightened. Pity. It looked such a pretty mouth too.

"So Mr. Carter," Samantha continued, ignoring the warning glances Trisha flashed at her, "being that you're a friend of Greg's and might know about such things, what you could do if you had a mind to, is point her in the direction of a good dude ranch. Somewhere she can get the full wild-west experience while she's here."

If he had a mind to. Cameron turned that idea over. If Trisha went anywhere with him he would have no mind at all, he was sure of it. Just the thought of being alone with her made his blood race and sent adrenaline surging as it did when he wrestled a steer.

"There's no need for that." Trisha's cheeks turned pink with embarrassment, or anger, he wasn't sure. "I can get brochures or something at a tourist office."

"Nonsense." Samantha ignored Trisha's pleadings. "If you want the real deal you go to the experts. Isn't that right, Mr. Carter?"

Cameron couldn't help himself. Trisha looked so darn cute, all fluffed up like a kitten having a hissy fit that words raced out of his mouth before his brain could change gear.

"Where and when can I pick you up tomorrow morning?"

"There really is no need," Trisha insisted. Her frustration at being out-maneuvered by Samantha showed in her narrowed eyes and down-turned mouth.

Samantha offered Cameron a business card.

"My office. Nine o'clock." The tone in her voice warned there would be no argument.

Cameron took the card and tucked it into his shirt pocket. Call him dumb, but tomorrow already looked pretty peachy. He grinned. "Who do I ask for?"

From the mulish look on her face, he knew he would not get the satisfaction of that piece of information from the girl sitting opposite him.

"Trisha Watts," Samantha answered sweetly.

"Nice to meet you, Ms. Watts." Cameron held out his hand and she reluctantly shook it. He sucked in a deep breath as their fingers locked, the warmth of her skin melding with his. "Tomorrow at nine it is."

Stars already dotted the darkening blanket of the night sky as he left the restaurant. He took off his hat and slapped it against his leg as he walked to his truck. What was he thinking?

He needed all his concentration for the next ten days of intense competition at the Stampede. Now he had offered his services to a true dude. Cute as all get out and spiky as a porcupine but still a dude. Not only that, a dude that set his pulse racing and made his heart thump like an old hay baling machine.

What the hell had he let himself in for?

Chapter Three

Music blasted from loudspeakers and vibrated through the floor, thumping in Cameron's ears. How anyone could work in this racket amazed him. People carrying clipboards, lamps, cameras rushed from one place to another somehow avoiding crashing into each other.

Nine o'clock sharp Samantha had insisted, yet at twenty minutes after the hour she and Trisha had still not arrived. Crushing disappointment pressed him into the sagging couch where he'd been invited to wait by a pint-sized assistant who introduced herself as Dee.

He spotted her wagging her finger at a technician. The tech appeared less than impressed as he pushed his headphones off his head and hung them around his neck. Tired of waiting, Cameron heaved himself off the couch. He made his way towards them through a mess of cables snaking their way across the floor.

"Tommy, you're not paid to think, you're paid to do. Just trust me on this one, okay?" The girl whirled around when Cameron tapped her on the shoulder.

"I'll wait outside," he said. "I'm in a no-parking zone and don't want a ticket."

Whatever her reply, he didn't hear it as he left the studio and hurried down the stairs.

Exiting the building into the alley behind it, he stood for a moment waiting for his head to clear, stunned by the heaviness in the pit of his stomach.

In spite of his reservations he'd wanted Trisha to be there. He'd wanted to see her again but fought the suspicion that she'd only agreed to go horseback riding to keep Samantha Monroe happy. With a sigh of resignation he grabbed the door handle of the truck. If something had happened to her, would she contact him and reschedule?

"Mr. Carter."

Relief flooded through him at the sound of Trisha's voice. He turned towards her, not caring if the grin on his face was goofy or not, but darn it, she made him feel good.

"Is the wild-west still open for business?" The pretty blush that colored her cheeks warred with the cool expression in her eyes. The tilt of her head emphasized her question but her apprehension showed in the way she caught her lower lip between her teeth.

He could be open for anything if she continued to chew her lip like that.

"Sorry we were late." Her blush deepened. "Punctuality isn't exactly one of Samantha's finer points."

"Well, you're here now and that's what matters seeing as it's you who wants the wild-west experience."

"Yes, about that." Trisha hesitated. "You really shouldn't go to any trouble on my behalf."

"Where I'm going to take you is no trouble at all, if you're still interested."

"It would appear I don't have much of a choice, Mr. Carter."

Her bluntness caught him off guard but he guided her round to the passenger side of his truck anyway.

"If we're to spend the day together, please call me Cameron."

Holding the door open for her, he caught a hint of her perfume as she clambered into the cab, fresh and sweet like the lilacs his mother once favored. Her fingers fumbled with the safety belt and he noticed how much they trembled. Not a good sign. He reached in and helped her fasten the buckle. He didn't want her to do anything that made her uncomfortable, but nor did he want to forego the pleasure of getting to know her. Sliding into his seat, he hardly dared believe she actually sat beside him and the truck hadn't yet moved an inch. He stared straight ahead as he fired up the engine, even though all he wanted was to sit and look at her. Darn it, what state would he be in after an hour or so of being at such close quarters with her?

"Where are we going?" Trisha asked once they were on the highway.

"Just a little place I know where there's a friendly horse or two and an easy trail."

"Really friendly?"

He heard the scepticism in her voice and knowing that she watched him, nodded his head.

"Absolutely. You'll get on just fine with Jack," Cameron assured her. "If you don't want to ride him, you don't have to."

"You'll probably think me silly."

"Nah. I heard you were from London and I'd probably balk at riding on one of your tube trains."

"That news travelled fast." Trisha pulled a face. "Hardly surprising, I suppose. And yes, the tube is an experience that's for sure. But you'd have to remove your hat."

"Oh no, not that." He grinned at her. "The hat stays put except for dinner and church."

It pleased him to see her mouth relax into something close to a smile and they drove on in almost comfortable silence.

Once they'd left the city limits behind them, Trisha watched the countryside roll by, one mile after another. Where she expected to see open grassland she saw softly swelling hills. The shoulder of one folded gently into another as they gradually rose to the serrated outline of the distant Rocky Mountains.

"I thought it would be flat." She waved an expressive hand at the scenery.

Cameron laughed. "You want flat, you go east onto the prairies. This is foothills country. Good grass, good water, good tree cover. You couldn't ask for better."

Just as she had a childlike urge to ask 'are we there yet', Cameron turned in at a freshly painted white gateway. The truck rattled over a metal grid and Trisha clenched her teeth. Trees shaded one side of the driveway while a neat corral fence lined the other. Ahead of them a barn stood off to one side but it was the jaw-dropping single-storey log house beyond it that caught her attention.

It could have come right out of a glossy home magazine. She immediately pictured curls of smoke rising from the chimney jutting out of one end of the roof. A fishbowl window above the solid entrance door shattered that cozy thought, as it gave the impression of keeping a wary eye on visitors. Large windows along the front of the house were shaded by the deep wrap-around veranda.

As soon as Cameron parked in front of the house two dogs came running from the shelter of the surrounding trees. He got out of the truck and Trisha watched him stroke their heads and gently fondle their ears.

This couldn't be the same guy she saw yesterday. That guy came across as a flippant jerk, but then she remembered the tenderness she'd sensed in his touch when they'd met again in the store. Her heart almost skipped a beat at the thought.

He pushed the dogs out of his way as he came casually around in front of the vehicle, as if not wanting to appear too eager to help her. What happened to the guy who brushed her off at the baggage carousel? Without thinking she twisted in her seat and put her hands on his shoulders but avoided looking at him. He settled his grip just above her waist.

Trisha took a deep breath as she let him lift her down. The warm pressure of his hands on her sides reassured her, but was it just coincidence that his thumbs were close to the underside of her breasts? A shiver of pleasant anticipation raised the small hairs on the back of her neck but as soon as her feet hit the ground, he let her go.

"Don't worry, they're friendly." Cameron gestured to the dogs, still bouncing around them. "This hound is Groucho and the blue heeler is Busby."

Trisha petted them as they nosed around her.

"Groucho, Busby, go lie down." Cameron pointed at the veranda. Both dogs trotted up the steps into the shade where they both lay down as commanded. Satisfied, Cameron turned to her. "This is your day, Trisha, so what would you like to do first?" His deep voice rumbled in her ears. "Meet the horses? Come in to the house and have a coffee?"

Trisha looked around her. Had she taken leave of her senses? The only other vehicle in sight was a battered old pickup truck parked beside the barn, a square bale of hay and a few planks of wood visible in its bed. She was alone in a remote location with a very large man whom she'd only met for a few moments the previous day. She hadn't even called Samantha to let her know they were leaving town.

And where exactly was she? She hadn't checked the time when they left, so had no idea how long the trip had been. An hour? Two? She cut a quick glance in Cameron's direction. That he waited patiently for her to make a decision showed the kind of consideration she barely gave herself, let alone expected from someone she'd just met.

Taking a deep breath in readiness to answer him, her nose detected a difference in the cologne to that he'd worn yesterday. Then a refreshingly light citrus spiked with an undertone of pepper had assailed her nostrils but today she detected the woodsy aromas of cedar and sandalwood. Whatever those fine tendrils of fragrance might be, she liked it a bit too much and couldn't imagine being anywhere else but close to him. No, she had nothing to fear from him she decided, only her treacherous self.

"A coffee would be nice," she murmured, still looking around. Cameron had mentioned horses, but there were none in the corral. Maybe they were in the barn.

"This way." He headed up the shallow veranda steps and opened the front door.

Trisha followed right behind him into a room brightened by sunlight. It flooded through the fishbowl window and warmed the stone tiled floor inside the door. Brightly patterned scatter rugs added a splash of color. A fireplace filled with ready-to-light logs, sat in a floor-to-ceiling river-stone chimney. A leather sofa, the color of old tobacco, faced the fireplace with matching chairs either side of it. If they were as comfortable as they looked, she'd never want to get out of them. Even the dining area looked comfortable with its solid looking oak table surrounded by ladder back chairs.

A great deal of care and consideration had gone in to creating an appearance of a homey ambiance yet the undisturbed air hung still and empty, as if it waited for a family to stir it up a little. She imagined the black granite counter tops littered with empty mugs and a vase of flowers on the end of the sturdy island bar.

"Is this your house?"

"It is."

Trisha didn't miss the pride in his voice or his smug smile as he invited her to take a seat. She boosted herself up on to a leather-upholstered bar stool at the island unit while Cameron measured coffee into the machine.

"It's very well designed." A quick survey of the kitchen told her the stainless steel appliances were all top quality.

"Thank you." Cameron collected mugs, cream and sugar and put them down in front of her. "It took a while. I worked on it when I had time but I'm happy with the result."

"You built it? On your own?" As soon as the words were out of her mouth she cringed at her own crassness. Of one thing she was already sure; this man could and would do anything he put his mind to.

"Mostly." Cameron hitched his hip onto the stool beside her. "Cut and seasoned the timber when I first bought the place and lived out of a trailer parked where the barn now is. Then I just worked on what I really wanted, picked the trades I needed and it all came together in its own good time."

She had a sudden image of him stripped to the waist, muscles flexing as he hammered nails into a log, his skin slicked with sweat and glistening in the sunshine. She smothered a sigh and pictured instead the house coming together, piece by piece, and understood his pride.

"I've never had my own home," she said. She hoped he missed the wistfulness she heard in her voice.

"Never?" Cameron raised a questioning eyebrow at her as he poured their coffee.

"Never. It would tie me down too much." Trisha slowly stirred cream into her mug, not sure how much to tell him, not sure how much he might understand of what her work entailed. "In between assignments I either crash with friends or go home to my parents. Pathetic, isn't it?"

"Not if that's what works for you. Do you enjoy what you do?"

His question leached into her brain. Did she? The jury was still out on that one. Photography had become a profitable substitute for a career that still sent her senses into overdrive when she thought of it. She missed the power and precision of her previous life, but there were too many risks involved, risks to life and limb and not only hers.

"It's been great," she said quickly, then caught herself and closed her mouth before she could reveal anything more. Had he noticed her use of the past tense? She lapsed into silence, startled by the direction her thoughts had taken her. Going back to what had been more a way of life than a career was not a good idea.

"Having a change of heart? Thinking about another career maybe?"

"Maybe." Trisha drew in her breath at Cameron's teasing tone and teased right back, "Maybe I'll become a cowgirl."

He laughed out loud at that. "A cowgirl who's ridden a camel and an elephant. Right."

"Don't forget the donkey." Trisha set the now empty coffee mug down, laid her palms on the edge of the island top and pushed herself up. "I'm ready for you to introduce me to Jack now. Maybe it's time to start my career change."

"Are you sure about this?"

Not trusting herself to give him a sensible answer, she nodded her head. He took hold of her hand as if it was the most natural thing to do and the shock of it zinged up her arm. The smile he gave her confirmed she must be in some alternate world. Why was he being so nice? Was he trying to make up for yesterday? And really, did he have to? If she were truthful, her dislike of flying had turned her into something of a snark.

As they entered the cool, dim interior of the barn she wrinkled her nose at the familiar sweet smell of hay and warm aroma of horses.

Cameron still held her hand, nor did she want him to let it go. The first few stalls on the left of the wide aisle were stacked with bales of hay and bags of wood shavings. To her right, saddles sat on wooden frames. Bridles, halters and other equipment whose purpose she could only guess at, hung from hooks on the wall. An ATV sat in the centre of what appeared to be a wash stall.

Attracted by the sound of their boots on the concrete floor, two horses looked out over their stall doors. They both nickered a soft welcome and Cameron said hello to both of them. He loosened his grip on her hand and smoothed the sleek brown neck of the horse closest to him.

"This is Anchorman. He's my top performer right now."

Across the aisle the other horse banged the side of the stall with an impatient hoof and tossed his head.

"Okay, Jack, quit making such a racket. I'm coming." Cameron clipped a rope to the horse's halter, opened the door and led him out.

"Trisha Watts, meet Jack." The horse nuzzled him as he spoke, then turned its head and sniffed Trisha's hand. "Jack's an old stager. He was the first horse I bought and trained myself and he's rock solid."

Trisha slid her hand along the horse's silky copper-colored neck and chuckled as Jack's rubbery lips plucked her sleeve. His gentleness encouraged her to run her fingers down the velvet softness of his white muzzle. She scratched him gently under his chin and Jack gave a soft sigh and dropped his head. His pleasure at this attention showed in his droopy lower lip and half closed eyes, all the signs of a relaxed and happy horse.

Cameron left them and headed towards the tack room. Trisha hadn't missed the puzzled frown on his face. She'd tried to give him the impression that she wasn't into horses or riding. Then she'd forgotten herself when she deftly found the sweet spot beneath Jack's chin. She knew Cameron had recognized that familiarity and hadn't expected it. If he glanced back over his shoulder now he'd see her talking softly to the horse and gently pulling one of its ears.

When he returned with the tack, Trisha stepped back to give him room to work. She watched him place a thick padded blanket on Jack's back then top it with the saddle.

"That looks heavy," she said.

"It has to be," Cameron explained as he hooked the stirrup onto the horn and reached under Jack's belly for the cinch. "Average weight for a roping saddle, which this is, is forty to fifty pounds. Not like those itty-bitty English saddles you're probably more familiar with. Shall we go?"

Trisha gave him a brief nod of agreement. Jack's hooves rang on the hard surface of the barn floor but changed to a soft shuffle in the dust as they walked out into the sunshine. Cameron said nothing as they continued towards the corral. With each step they took Trisha tensed. Was she really going to do this? Was she really going to get back on a horse?

"We'll start in the round pen."

Trisha looked at the arrangement of fence panels Cameron indicated. She opened the gate for him and stood to one side so he and Jack could enter. She heard the slap and creak of leather as Cameron dropped the reins, adjusted the saddle and tightened the cinch.

She stood quite still. The warm breeze played across her face and teased the hair on the back of her neck. Jack dropped his hip and rested a hind hoof. His tail swished across his hind leg and the bug he dislodged flew up and into her face. Brushing it away she became aware that Cameron watched her and lifted her eyes to his.

For a blink of time their gazes caught and held. She knew her cheeks to be pale, knew her features to be rigid with tension. She expected to see censure in his expression, disappointment at her feebleness but there was none. A muscle twitched in her jaw as she gritted her teeth.

"You don't have to do this," he said quietly.

Her clenched fists rested against her thighs. "Then I'd have to admit to Samantha that I chickened out. No thank you."

"Okay, Trisha, if you're sure."

"I'm sure." She couldn't help snapping at him. Why did he have to be so damn understanding? "Let's get on with it."

Trisha saw his mouth settle into a thin line at her sharp retort and was immediately sorry for it. He'd been finagled into giving her a unique western experience. At the very least she could try to appreciate it. She gave herself a mental shake and looked up at the sound of his voice.

"I want you to hold the saddle horn with your left hand, the back of the saddle with your right hand. Then you're going to put your left foot into the stirrup and boost yourself up off your right foot and swing that leg clear over the saddle. Got that?"

She took a step closer to Jack, fighting the tremors that threatened to engulf her. She closed her eyes. Breathe in, breathe out, she told herself.

You are getting on a horse for the first time in two years and nothing more than just sitting on it is expected of you.

Cameron held the big box stirrup for her. She looked at it as if it was the head of a snake with its fangs about to sink into her booted foot, but she shook the image away. Settling the toe of her boot right where it should be, she swallowed her fear and swung into the saddle.

For once she was able to look down at Cameron. Doubt lurked in the expression in his eyes. She couldn't blame him for that. Samantha's insistence that he find her a dude ranch did neither of them any favors. An overwhelming urge to touch him, to commiserate with him, didn't help her confusion. Just where had that come from anyway?

Her fingers came alive where he touched them as he showed her how to hold the split reins. His hand warmed her knee where he steadied her as he walked with Jack around the pen. A sensation of being cast adrift washed over her when he let her go.

"Just give him a nudge with your heels to keep him moving," he called out to her. "We might make a cowgirl of you yet. Keep him going."

After watching her for a few more moments, Cameron turned and headed back to the barn. Trisha watched him walk away, her insides turning to mush at the sight of his broad shoulders, the twitch of his hips and the shape of his long legs. If she couldn't keep her eyes off him now this was going to be one doozey of a day.

"What the hell am I going to do, Jack?" The horse snorted and shook his head, making his bit jingle. She managed a shaky laugh and patted his neck. "You're no help at all, buddy."

Jack continued to plod around the pen and Trisha found herself more comfortable with every step he took. Gradually relaxing into the saddle, she didn't notice Cameron riding up until she heard the gate rattle.

He sat the brown horse as easily as if he'd been born there, looking so good her mouth watered. He reached over and swung the gate open, holding it for her as she guided Jack through it.

She dared not glance at him. Yesterday he'd put her on edge with his quick grin and smart remarks. Today he'd touched something in her and awakened a sudden, intense need to be held and cared for. How long had it been since she'd experienced that? The man who had shown her all the delights of a loving relationship had proved to be a cheat and a liar and she hadn't risked losing her heart again. She hoped Cameron wouldn't see her confusion and think her inept but he mistook her hesitancy for apprehension.

"We'll take it nice and steady," he assured her. "Most places we can ride side by side but where the trail narrows just let Jack tuck in behind me."

Trisha nodded, not trusting herself to speak. This man made her think of sharing a warm bed on a cold night or sitting on a deck in quiet companionship. Beyond those thoughts were naked limbs and hot, heavy sex. She blinked away the image and kept her eyes on Jack's neck, on the grass, anywhere but on Cameron. She didn't dare let him see her attraction to him. It wasn't only his quiet words and apparent understanding, more the look and scent of him. The quiet confidence he wore like a birthright seemed to enfold her too. As she relaxed, she started to look about and take in her surroundings.

They were riding along a wide green corridor between stands of trees. The breeze rustled the leaves on their branches and ahead of them the trail started to rise. Beyond the rise the peaks of the Rocky Mountains stood out sharp and clear against an azure blue sky.

Then Cameron halted and held a finger to his lips. She looked to where he pointed, delighted to see a small herd of deer.

"Whitetail," he whispered. He nudged his horse on and Jack followed, striding out so smoothly that Trisha could have been sitting in a comfy chair.

"You're doing well," Cameron said after watching her for a moment. "How long is it since you rode a horse?"

She shrugged, pretending an indifference she didn't feel. "A couple of years or thereabouts. Now I just take photos of them."

"Why?"

His question caught her off guard. She opened her mouth to speak but closed it again as she paused for thought, frowning as she did so. Why did she like taking photographs of horses so much? No one had ever asked her that question and she turned it over in her mind before giving an answer.

"Because I get satisfaction from capturing an image of their power and freedom," she offered and fell silent as Cameron headed into the trees.

Just as he'd said, Jack tucked in and plodded along nose-to-tail behind the lead horse. The trail dropped down a steep incline and she instinctively leaned back, feeling the curve of the saddle cradling her behind and imagining it was Cameron's hands.

There was no point wishing for what couldn't be and she blinked the image away. Emerging from the cover of the trees into a mountain meadow, all thoughts fled from her mind at the sight that met her eyes and she couldn't help but smile with pleasure at the view in front of her.

"Quite something isn't it?" Cameron looked pleased. "It impresses most folks I bring up here."

Cool, clean air as heady as champagne filled her lungs with every breath she took and she looked about her again. Cameron had dismounted and his horse was already tearing greedily at the long grass.

Following his example she swung out of the saddle, stepping down from the stirrup as easily if it had been a stair tread. "I really should have brought my camera."

"Why didn't you?" Cameron took a canteen out of his saddle bag and offered it to her.

"For once I decided to take a real day off." She took the canteen, aware of his fingers folded around it, careful not to touch them even though she found she wanted that connection however meager.

She closed her eyes as she sipped the cool liquid. Relishing the sensation of it filling and refreshing her mouth, she swallowed it slowly before handing the canteen back. Cameron's fingers brushed over hers, daring to do what she had not. Was that touch purely accidental or had he done it deliberately?

He tipped his head back and took a long pull on the canteen. Trisha watched the muscles in his throat working with each swallow. She tore her gaze away when he licked a drop of water from his lips and resisted an overwhelming desire to reach out and touch him.

"Come and sit down," he invited. He walked a little way down the slope to where a long slab of rock jutted out from the hillside. Trisha joined him. The heat from the sun-warmed stone seeped through her jeans along with that from his body where his leg rested easily against hers.

She licked her lips, wanting to say something, not knowing what they could talk about, only aware that her body betrayed every resolve she had drilled into her mind. She wanted to touch him, to have him touch her. And after the touch ...? She pressed her lips together.

"So how long are you staying in Calgary?"

His quiet question made her jump and she quickly gathered her thoughts.

"Until the Wednesday after Stampede finishes," she answered. "Then I go back to England to finish off my Horses in Sport assignment."

"If you're not so keen on riding, why would you even take an assignment like that?"

"It's my job and I'm very good at it." Trisha lay back and closed her eyes. Sunlight warmed her face, seeped into her skin allowing her fears and doubts to gradually slip away. For now, this moment, she didn't want to think, only experience what it was to just be.

"What sports are you going to include?" His soft voice drifted into her ears.

"Thoroughbred racing, trotting horses, then the bucking broncs, chuck wagon teams and barrel racing horses at the Stampede. When I go home I'll be spending some time with a good friend, Camille Langdon, to interview her about her horses. She's the current European three-day event champion."

Trisha didn't add the fact that she had once been a contender for that title. That life, with all its marvelous highs and dreadful lows, now seemed so far away.

"Are you writing this for a magazine?"

"Yes, the Equine World annual edition which will come out early December in time for Christmas."

Silence fell between them again and Cameron lay back on the rock beside her.

"I guess you're doing double duty then, writing that article and judging Ms. Monroe's competition."

"I'm not judging anything," Trisha corrected him. "I'll just be helping sort through some photographs of male models she's interested in signing up for the agency."

"How'd you meet her?"

His voice came from deep in his chest and Trisha turned her head just enough for him to be in her line of sight. He'd tipped his hat over his eyes and the brim covered all but the curve of his jaw from his ear lobe to the point of his chin. Dark hair curled at the vee of his open shirt. Her fingers itched to pop a button and she wanted nothing more than to trail her fingertips over his bare body. Looking away, she sat up and curled her fingers into her palms to make her hands behave.

"At the Toronto Fashion Week a couple of years ago." Trisha thought back to that day. "We quite literally bumped into each other. We both apologized at the same time, burst into laughter at such a silly situation and fell into an instant friendship. We worked together for the whole of fashion week and then a few more weeks after that. We've kept in touch ever since."

Yanking a blade of grass out of the ground Trisha twisted it nervously in her fingers.

Well, that was brilliant. He should be all agog for her next astounding bit of conversation.

Cameron propped himself up on one elbow. "How did you go from photographing horses to fashion?"

"A British designer brought out a line of riding-inspired fashions and I got the assignment." She'd also been asked to model but had declined that invitation and chose not to share that information now. She fell silent again and stared at the tree covered slopes around her.

"You don't seem very comfortable with me," Cameron mused.

With a whoosh of breath she hadn't been aware she'd been holding, Trisha dropped her chin on her chest. She wanted to get very comfortable with him but wouldn't risk him guessing her runaway thoughts.

"I'm sorry, I'm being so rude." She laughed ruefully. "I must still be tired from my flight."

He nodded at that. "Guess that would do it. Plus the altitude takes a bit of adjusting to."

Her eyes widened in surprise. "Altitude?"

"Sure. Calgary's three thousand feet above sea level." He shrugged. "Give or take a few feet and we're higher still right here."

He stood up and dusted his rear end, slapped his hat into place and then held his hand out. Trisha took it and he pulled her up. Once they were mounted again he headed down the slope. Trisha could barely see a path yet Cameron's horse picked its way easily. She looked out over the rise and fall of the surrounding terrain. No sign of a road anywhere, only tree-covered slopes and below them a valley of wind ruffled grass.

"So how much of this land belongs to you and what do you do with it?" She swayed comfortably in the saddle as Jack navigated the narrow trail.

"I've got two hundred acres, most of it to grow hay for the horses I raise and train. I hold one training clinic a month at my place through the summer, as well as at horse shows and rodeos." Cameron glanced over his shoulder at her. "Come winter I'll board some extra horses and the barn's often full then. My horses are raised to work, but we use them for sport too. Without them we wouldn't be steer wrestling. I know a few bronc riders, chuck wagon drivers and barrel racers too. Let me know if you need any introductions."

They reached the bottom of the slope and came to a shallow creek. Cameron's horse waded in without any hesitation, followed by Jack. As they came up the bank on the far side both horses stopped, heads up, ears pricked. Their breath huffed out of their distended nostrils and they shuffled their feet, bumping nervously into each other.

"Uh-oh," Cameron drew his rifle from its scabbard. "Something's up. Stay behind me."

The unmistakable metallic snick of a round being chambered turned Trisha's veins to ice. The horses continued to snort and move restlessly, both spooked by something only they could sense. She looked up and down the creek.

"What is it?" Fear made her voice quake.

Cameron scanned the trees before pointing to a branch just above head height several feet away.

"Cougar," he said.

A tawny body stretched along the length of a branch. Its deep growl became a hissing snarl and escalated in volume to a bone-chilling screech. Long canines and a pink tongue showed against a white, bewhiskered face.

"Damn cat." Sunlight glinted off the long, sleek barrel as Cameron lifted the rifle, took aim at the branch above the cougar's head and fired.

The sharp crack of the shot crashed into Trisha's ear drums. Acrid smoke filled her nostrils. Cold sweat broke out on her forehead and familiar shakes took hold of her body. She barely noticed the lithe form bounding away from them. Her head spun and her stomach clenched. Her lungs burned, cutting off her breath.

Drawn into a vortex of confusion, she spiraled down into that place she didn't want to be, a place of chaos and pain ending in complete and utter darkness.

Chapter Four

Cameron slid the rifle back into the scabbard, swung off his horse and caught Trisha's limp body as she slumped in the saddle. Easing her to the ground, he cradled her in his arms. He'd so badly wanted to hold her, but not like this. Not with her out cold and unresponsive.

Taking off her hat he smoothed her hair back from her white face, frowning as his fingers ran over a narrow ridge of pink, puckered scar tissue on her hairline. It ran from the centre of her forehead to just above her right ear.

He frowned as he tried to imagine what may have caused it. She must have suffered some major event to make her to faint like this. The cougar, the sound of the rifle discharging, the scuffling of the frightened horses could have scared her into thinking she might be injured again.

He rocked her to and fro, rubbing the backs of his fingers over her cheeks until her color returned and her eyelids fluttered.

"Don't be in a hurry to move," he said quietly as she opened her eyes. "You've had a shock, but you're fine. We're all fine."

She blinked at him as if trying to remember where she was then looked around. Jack and

Anchorman grazed nearby, a sure sign that the danger, at least for now, had passed. She groaned as she sat up and held her head.

"I'm so sorry," she whispered.

She sniffed and he hoped she wasn't going to cry. He was no good at dealing with tears. He pulled her against his chest and without thinking dropped a kiss on top of her head. The contact of his lips on the softness of her hair resulted in her stiffening in his arms and he reluctantly let her go.

"You've got nothing to be sorry for." He wasn't sure if it she was frightened of him or the cougar.

She scrubbed her hand across her face to brush away the moisture forming on her lower lashes. "Did you kill it?"

"Nope, scared it off is all."

"Well," She scrambled awkwardly to her feet. "I wanted a wild-west experience, I guess I got it."

"That's a good way to look at it." Cameron picked up her hat and handed it to her, but she swayed as she took it. "Here, you'd best sit down again."

He caught her by the arms and steadied her as she sank into the grass and put her head between her knees. Cameron pulled off his bandana, soaked it in the creek and wrung it out before placing the cool wadded cloth on the back of her neck. She flinched, but held it in place while he fetched the canteen then sat down beside her and handed it to her.

Trisha took a deep pull on it and licked the moisture off her lips before screwing the cap back on. He nearly choked at the sight of that little pink tongue at the corner of her mouth. Was it as sweet as it looked? He turned away before the temptation to find out made him pull her into his arms and kiss her senseless. Last thing she needed after so severe a shock was to know the effect she had on him.

"Thank you for being so understanding."

The quaver in her voice cut him to the core. "Think nothing of it. While you're with me, that's my job. Are you ready to go now?"

A tremulous smile wavered on her lips and she nodded. Cameron helped her mount Jack, his pulse racing, his mind reeling. She'd been petrified but now tried to put on a brave face. Why? Most girls he knew would either have been screaming and running away as fast as they could, or shooting right along side of him. Yet Trisha seemed to be drawing on every nerve she possessed to play the whole incident down.

He swung up into Anchorman's saddle and headed the horse towards home.

"Does something like that often happen?" Trisha moved Jack alongside him.

"No, but it doesn't hurt to know what's out there." Cameron sensed she was still shaken and saved telling her about bears and bull elk for another day. If there was one. He almost sighed with disappointment when they halted outside his barn. He didn't want this day to be over.

Trisha watched him as he stripped the saddles off the horses.

"They're cool enough that we can turn them out right away," he said and handed her both sets of reins.

She seemed quite comfortable as she led the horses to the corral. He opened the gate for her and showed her how to slip the bridles off, although he had a sense she knew what to do. Both horses sank to their knees and stretched out to roll their sweaty backs in the dirt, then scrambled to their feet and shook off the dust.

Trisha chuckled as she watched them wander away and begin grazing. "So much for their after work shower."

Cameron agreed and smiled at her, relieved that she appeared to have recovered herself. As they walked towards the house he noticed a strained look on her face and her tight little steps.

"Let me guess," he said as they reached the veranda steps. "Bathroom break?"

She nodded with apparent relief.

"The door at the end of the veranda is to my bedroom. Go in there and the bathroom's at the back on your right."

Trisha followed his directions and almost stopped on the threshold at the sight of his king sized four poster bed. As she got closer to it she could see intricate carvings of animals and trees on the posts. Without thinking she reached up to touch the post nearest to her.

Her fingertips traced the outline of a deer's antlers, then a tree trunk with roughened surface to emulate bark with its knots and swirls and little ridges. She curled her whole hand around the post and the fine edges of the design pressed into her palm. Her spread fingers read the rest of the patterns but then she connected with a hard, satiny smooth surface.

The image that came into her mind brought heat to her face and tightness to her lungs. Would Cameron be this hard, this smooth, if she had her fingers curled around him? Would he close his eyes or watch her? Would he like it if she closed her hand and tightened her grip? She stepped back as if she'd been scalded and hurried into the bathroom.

Catching sight of herself in the mirror, she grimaced. Tear tracks plowed furrows down her dusty cheeks. She put her hand up to cover the place where Cameron had touched her as if to capture his caress. Even in her state of shock his gentleness had touched her heart and jolted her back to full consciousness.

She closed her eyes in an effort to recall the worried expression in Cameron's eyes but older images flickered across the inside of her lids. Blue sky. Crowds of people. The tree-trunk. A grunt of effort from the horse beneath her. Her counselor's voice echoed in her head. Breathe in slowly. Take the breath deep into your lungs. Let your thoughts go on an exhale. Watch them riding your breath out of your body until your mind is clear. Breathe in a long, deep fresh breath and imagine your perfect place where you are safe and happy.

Did she even deserve to have that? The face she showed the world told one thing, her demons told her another.

With a sigh of resignation she took off her hat and placed it on the counter, turned on the tap and let it run until the water was just warm. Scooping it into her hands she splashed the dust away before grabbing a towel and blotting her face dry. But she couldn't wash away the burning memory of being in Cameron's arms, a memory that colored her cheeks as she remembered the gentle pressure of his fingers on her face and the flare of passion she saw in his expression.

The expression on her own face as she looked into the mirror again surprised her. Sure, her eyes, nose and mouth were right where they should be. But how could her eyes be so deep a green? Could thoughts of Cameron have caused her pupils to dilate with arousal? Why did her lips look so full and plump as if they'd been thoroughly kissed?

Her skin tingled and a delicious quiver rippled through every muscle at the recollection of his hands on her body. Her breasts tightened and her lace bra chafed her hardened nipples into tight buds. Cameron filled her mind and she no longer denied how much she wanted him to fill her body.

Her breath shortened and she gasped in surprise as pressure built between her thighs and tightened in her lower belly. With a deep groan she sank onto the edge of the bath. Using the cool curve of the porcelain for balance she pressed a hand against her chest as if to slow the crazy rhythm of her heart. She could not be having an orgasm in a stranger's bathroom. She just could not.

At last her pulse slowed, her breathing became more even, huffing in little puffs between her lips as it returned to normal.

Normal. What was that anyway? And what the hell had just happened to her? How could her body so inexorably betray every resolve she'd made? And if every nerve could be shredded just by thinking about Cameron, what would it be like if ...?

No. She couldn't go there. She stood up and ran the tap again.

Cold water this time. Really cold water to cool her still hot face and neck.

Now she had to go back outside and face him. She couldn't, wouldn't let him see the effect he'd had on her.

She pulled her shoulders back, stood up straight and ran her fingers through her hair to straighten it before replacing her hat.

Feeling anything but confident, she made her way back outside.

* * *

Cameron leaned against the veranda post. She sure was taking her sweet time. But that gave him the chance to try and figure out why she ruffled his feathers so. Just as he was thinking he should check on her, she came out of his bedroom, strolled along the veranda and leaned against the post opposite him.

"That's some bed back in there."

Her eyes glowed green-as-moss in the late afternoon sunshine, highlighting her pink cheeks and moist, puffy lips. If he didn't know better, he'd say that Ms. Watts had been well and truly bedded on it.

"Another of my specs. Think that was after Abilene." He tried to not think of them together in that bed. His groin tightened and he crossed his legs. Now was not the time to let a boner get the better of him. He saw her eyebrow lift and his heart lifted with it. "Yeah, won the steer wrestling at the rodeo there a few years ago."

He pictured another kind of wrestling now.

"So that's what you meant when you said your house came together in its own good time. You used your winnings to build it."

Cameron took a deep breath, knocked sideways at the appreciative light in her eyes and nodded. "I did."

"Do you still steer wrestle?"

He couldn't ignore the slight huskiness in her voice. It played across his tingling nerves and made him picture rumpled sheets and gentle candlelight but he pushed that thought away as he attempted to answer her question.

"It's hard to give it up." How could he convey the adrenaline rush that came from chasing a steer and having a good horse beneath him? How could he explain all the elements of those few crucial seconds between winning and losing? The words seemed beyond him. He shrugged and scratched the back of his neck. "Depending on the weather you're covered in dust or mud for hours. You sleep in your truck or trailer or the handiest hotel and swear by every bruise and aching muscle you'll give it up. But there you are next go round, waiting to chase the dream of a big win all over again."

"You're competing at the Calgary Stampede?"

Damn. Why did her eyes have to be so darn intense? He took a deep breath.

"That's the big one everyone wants to win. Besides, it's the best advertisement for my horses." His gaze settled on her face again, but she turned away as if avoiding his eyes. What didn't she want him to see? "Hey, are you hungry? We could go into town and grab a bite."

Going to town was not back to Calgary as he knew she expected but a thirty minute trip in the opposite direction. Once they hit the small town's limits he slowed down and drove past a row of stores fronted by false facades and boardwalks.

"Does this even qualify as a town?" Trisha asked. "It looks like it could have starred in some old western movie."

He laughed at that. "Actually it has. The garages and feed merchants on the other side of the street have played their part, too."

He pulled up in front of a diner with the name 'Tumbleweed' in faded lettering above the door, assuring her it was better than it looked as they got out of the truck.

An old fashioned bell above the lintel announced their entrance. Large overhead industrial shades spilled light over the counter and onto the plank floor, creating shadows that made it impossible to see anything clearly. Directional lighting fixtures around the walls illuminated a ceiling dark with age and the remnants of cigarette and cigar smoke.

Cameron waved to the pony-tailed waitress behind the counter and headed for an empty booth. The banquette, upholstered in tired red leatherette, gave a small sigh of protest as Trisha sat down. Perched on stools at the counter, a few customers turned to watch her with undisguised interest. Her cheeks flamed, even though she realized any newcomer would probably receive the same attention.

A waitress hurried over and handed them menus. "Hi, Cameron. Haven't seen you in a while."

"Hey, Star. Been getting ready for Stampede," he offered. "I'll have my usual steak and a coffee."

"What about you, hon?" Star's voice sounded scratchy and tired, over used from asking the same question a hundred times a day.

"What's good on the menu?" Cameron watched Trisha run her finger down the list. He nearly laughed at the puzzled expression on her face when she stopped and asked, "What, exactly, is a Denver sandwich?"

"That would be eggs scrambled with ham, onion, green pepper and served between two slices of toasted bread," Star explained. "Guess you don't have them in England, huh?"

Trisha shook her head and grinned. "No, we don't. So what would you recommend from this menu?"

"Honestly?" Star tapped the end of her pencil against her chin. "Depends what mood our chef Tank's in. Today he's good, so pretty much anything."

A shout from the far end of the counter caught the waitress's attention and she frowned at the man propped up beside an antique cash register. Light glinted off the ornate chasing on its back and side panels and the last purchase of $2.99 showed clearly under the glass dome.

"You mind your manners, Brodie," Star called back. "I'll be with you when I'm done here."

"Doesn't matter what mood Tank's in." Cameron explained. "He can always grill up a perfect steak. That's why it's my usual order."

"Then I'll have steak, medium well done, with a baked potato, please."

"You got it, hon." Star took the menus back, scribbled on her pad and went to talk to the man she called Brodie.

64

"Brodie can be a bit rowdy, but he's a good guy," Cameron said. "He's always hustling the wait staff. I think it's kind of a sport for him now. He used to rodeo, but got busted up one too many times."

"Are you afraid that will happen to you?" Trisha placed her elbows on the table and rested her chin on her intertwined fingers. She sat facing the door. The last of the afternoon sunshine played across her face, highlighting her interested expression.

Cameron swallowed the groan in his throat. There it was again, that slow surge in his groin that now swelled uncomfortably against his jeans. He shifted on the banquette, tried to ignore the signals his body sent him and shook his head.

"Calgary will be my last rodeo." Finally admitting it out loud cemented his decision. "I'm thirty five going on sixty eight. At least that's what it feels like some mornings. If I hit the big one I can go out on top. The winnings will get me the quarter horse stud I have my eye on. Then I'll concentrate on my horse business."

He stopped talking as Star arrived with their orders and placed them on the table, topped up their coffees and left them to it.

"And no-one knows about this yet?"

Cameron knew the journalist in Trisha would sense a story he wasn't quite ready to tell. "Only you and my hazer, Larry."

"What's a hazer?"

He caught his disbelief before he opened his mouth. Of course she wouldn't know the term. "When a steer comes out of the chute, the wrestler is on one side and the hazer on the other to keep it straight for the wrestler to catch. A good hazer is as priceless as a good horse."

"Oh, I see."

Did she? He hoped she'd missed the regret he was unable to keep out of his voice. Giving up the rodeo life still didn't sit well with him but at least he'd been able to make the decision for himself. When she'd done eating, she laid her knife and fork down and looked up.

The intensity in her green-eyed glance made Cameron's blood buzz like traffic on a freeway but the noisy jangle of the bell over the door saved him from making a fool of himself.

"Well, hell." He waved a hand at the newcomers filing into the diner. "Looks like tonight's going to be a Howlin' at the Moon jam session."

The men in the group carried guitars, a double bass and microphones to the back of the diner. Two girls, with the help of another two men from seats at the counter, made short work of setting up a five-piece band in the corner. Once the mics were set up, the guitars tuned and a drummer warming up on his cajon box drum, couples began to take to the floor.

"Local group." Cameron's voice rose above the music. "Every chance they get they come here and play. It's their way of saying thanks to the folks in town who supported them when they first started."

One of the girls stepped up to the microphone and began singing in a pure, clear voice. When the number came to a close the diner echoed with appreciative applause. Surprised at the volume of it, Trisha looked around. As well as the people inside the diner, many more gathered around the open door.

There was more applause as the band started up again, this time with one of the men leaning in to share the mic with the girl. They sang a tender duet of lost love and broken hearts, of stars and moonlit roads. Trisha found her foot tapping to the beat and joined in the applause when the number ended.

"Would you like to dance?"

She hesitated but the warm look in Cameron's eyes made her want to melt into his arms. He couldn't know what he was asking of her but she nodded her agreement. "If you don't mind having your toes trodden on. Dancing isn't one of my talents."

"The boots can take it and the two-step is easy." Cameron stood up and held out his hand.

For a moment her hesitation persisted then she slid out of the booth and put her hand in his. His fingers closed gently around hers. The heat and strength of that tenuous contact made her feel precious and protected. How could that be? Her pulse quickened as he led her towards the dance floor.

"Can you quick step?" he asked as his left arm circled her waist.

"Yes," she whispered as he turned her expertly into the corner of the floor.

"So you know the quick step rhythm is slow-slow, quick-quick slow?"

"Yes," Trisha whispered again, her tongue thick against the roof of her mouth.

"The two-step is the reverse." Cameron's breath, warm in the shell of her ear, raised goose-bumps on her arms. Her knees weakened. "It's quick-quick, slow-slow. Quick-quick, slow-slow."

Under his expert tuition Trisha followed him with ease. He spun her around and twisted her under his arm. How long had it been since she'd been so relaxed and enjoyed herself so much?

The tempo changed from the speedy two-step to a slow waltz. Cameron held her closer and she rested her cheek against the soft fabric of his shirt. The solid muscles of his chest pressed against her breasts, his firm thighs nudged hers as he continued to guide her around the floor. His arm tightened about her and she relaxed into him, a smile lingering on her face as his fingers tightened around hers.

A tremor ran through her. Yesterday morning she had wished to never see him again. Today she wished she wasn't so attracted to him. His muscles weren't built in a gym nor did his tan come out of a bottle. What she felt went far beyond his physicality. She knew she could trust him with her life. He'd already proved that. But if she let her guard down, would he judge her? Or would he, instead, help her to forget, help her past the nightmare that still haunted her?

The girl with the clear voice sang something about breathing and Trisha did just that. She breathed in the muted notes of his cedar and sandalwood cologne, his faint musky body smell and beneath all that the lemon of laundry detergent. The thought of Cameron doing something as mundane as laundry brought a new smile to her lips. She closed her eyes and just swayed with him.

"Uh, Trisha ..."

She looked up with a start. The music had stopped and the floor had cleared of dancers. One of the onlookers, with an amused grin on his face, started slow clapping then stepped up and punched Cameron lightly on the shoulder.

"Time was the ladies fell at your feet," the man said with a chuckle. "Seems like they just fall asleep on you now. You losin' your touch, or what?"

"Oh, I've embarrassed you." A blush rose up Trisha's neck and heated her cheeks. Her hands flew to her face to cover her dismay.

"Take a lot to do that." Cameron gently took her elbow and steered her back to the booth. "Looks like you're tired, so I think it's time I took you home."

Home. Such a simple word but she knew it took more than four walls and a roof to make one. It took people to make a home, people who loved one another, who argued and fell out with each other and then made up again. Looking around the diner she saw honest faces filled with genuine appreciation of the place they were in and the people they were with.

Not at all like her home where life seemed to revolve around horses not people. She knew her parents loved her, but her mother had paid more attention to a horse's scratched knee than to any injury Trisha might suffer. Her father spent time away from home training riders or, if they came to him, they littered the house like wayward kittens. Between them all she grew up almost undetected until her father, recognizing her potential, gave her his undivided attention. Attention that she at first relished and then became bound by and resented.

Thinking about her family and what might have been, brought unexpected tears to Trisha's eyes. Right now she missed her parents, the horses, the dogs and all their staff. In a word, she felt bereft. The bleakness of it washed over her and she had to blink away the tears as they said goodnight to Star.

"It got a bit warm in there," Cameron commented as they walked outside into the rapidly cooling night air.

Trisha said nothing, not wanting the reality that was her life to break the magic of the evening.

They walked without further conversation to his truck. Cameron unlocked the door and helped her in, then reached behind the seat and pulled out a blanket.

"You might need this," he said as he draped it over her shoulders. "The truck'll take a few minutes to warm up."

He slid into the driver's seat, fitted the key into the ignition and turned it. Trisha couldn't take her eyes off each movement he made.

The engine caught, turned over. Cameron waited until the motor ran smoothly before reversing carefully out into the street. He slid a CD into the tray in the dashboard and soft country and western music filtered through the cab.

Trisha snuggled deeper into the warmth of the blanket, relaxed as the heater kicked in wafting warmth over her feet. As the truck gathered speed, the lights from the store fronts they passed blurred in her vision until she gave in and closed her eyes. Lulled by the throb of the motor and hum of wheels on the hard-top road, she soon drifted into sleep.

* * *

Cameron looked across at her. Her head rolled loosely against the headrest with the motion of the truck. He didn't want her jolted awake, but neither did he like the other option that came to mind.

He'd risked enough tonight by asking her to dance. He liked the feel of her in his arms way too much, and what he now considered would put him on a slippery slope to things he shouldn't think about at all.

"Hot damn," he muttered. There was no way he could drive her all the way back to Calgary tonight.

Her head bumped again and he muttered another curse. She needed to be in bed, and the closest one around was his. If he tried hard enough, he might even buy that reasoning. He glanced across at her as he slowed for the turn into his driveway. She barely moved and only grunted slightly as he came to a stop.

Both dogs were on the veranda but he shushed them as he went to open the door to his bedroom. In a few strides he was beside his bed and turned back the comforter. He returned to the truck and lifted Trisha, blanket and all, up into his arms. Her head drooped on his shoulder but he could hear her snoring softly. That strangely intimate little sound made him hold her closer as he carried her to the bed where he carefully laid her down.

He wanted to lie down with her. Wanted to hold her close against his body. Hoped she wouldn't be scared when she woke up and would return his kisses when he offered them. But he wouldn't risk it, couldn't. She looked so frail but he sensed she struggled to maintain a balance between hard-nosed edginess and near panic. What had happened to her? She knew how to handle a horse however hard she tried to hide it. The way she sat into the saddle spoke of an old familiarity, yet her fear of mounting Jack had been as obvious as if she'd screamed at him.

She murmured a protest but didn't wake as he tugged off her boots. He pulled the comforter up around her and dimmed the bedside light, not wanting her to be scared if she woke up and didn't know where the hell she was. He leaned against the carved post at the end of the bed, finally admitting what had been bugging him all day.

Of all the girls he had dated over the years, the girls he'd loved and left with no hard feelings or regrets, this girl was different. Maybe it was her green eyes or the flash of auburn in her dark brown hair. Maybe it was her long, lean body and the knowledge that it would fit with his. Damn, but everything about her struck him as right. Maybe that was why he wanted to sooth away all the fears he sensed she harbored.

Common sense hit him square in the face. She knew nothing about ranching and came from a totally different world than his. If that wasn't a recipe for disaster he didn't know what was.

He scrubbed a hand over his face.

Whichever way he looked at it, he couldn't make sense of it. For whatever reason Trisha Watts had come into his life, for now she was in his bed.

Alone.

Chapter Five

The sky could not have been bluer or provided such a perfect backdrop ...

Her eyes flew open but she couldn't see anything. Where was she? Where was Del? She grabbed for his mane but instead of tightly bound braids her fingers connected with a soft, downy comforter. What the heck? She pushed her hair out of her eyes and looked around in panic.

She was in a bedroom, but whose bedroom? And where was it? Grabbing the edge of the comforter and pulling it around her, she scooted back to cower against the head of the bed. She covered her face with her hands, moaning softly behind them. She peered through her fingers as she felt the edge of the bed dip as someone sat down. Who was that guy? He wasn't Tony.

"Where's Tony?" she demanded.

Cameron caught her hands. "Sweetheart, who's Tony?"

"Tony's my, my ..."

Cameron watched her panic morph into confusion then awareness as her breathing slowed. She closed her eyes and covered her face again, shaking her head.

"Hey, come here." Cameron took her into his arms and held her close, stroking her back and allowing her time to fully wake up, gently rocking her as she clung to him.

He'd bunked on a couch in the family room last night but, unable to sleep, he'd run over their day together. By every indication, from instinctively knowing where best to scratch Jack to her deep natural seat, she had to be an experienced horsewoman. Samantha had alluded to the fact that Trisha hadn't ridden a horse in a while. What was the reason for that? Why had she admitted to riding other animals but not horses?

He'd heard her muttering in the night and padded quietly on bare feet through to the bedroom, watching her as she slept. Whatever she dreamt about made her draw her brows together in a deep frown. Her head had moved restlessly on the pillow, her fingers flickered and twitched, and then, with a deep sigh, she'd settled into a deeper level of sleep. He'd let his gaze roam over her slight shape before he'd gone back to the couch. He couldn't let whatever affected her bother him, but that was getting harder and harder to do.

"I'm sorry," she whispered. "I sometimes have nightmares."

"I guess." He continued to hold her, listening to her breathing steady into its regular rhythm and sensed when she was ready to pull away from him. Reluctant to let her go, he watched her throw back the comforter and edge her legs off the bed. She stood up and looked down at her crumpled clothes.

"God, I wish I had something clean." Her shirt had horse slobber down the front of it and her jeans were truly grubby. She swiped her hands over the wrinkles.

"Best I can offer is laundry facilities if you'd like," Cameron said.

"Perhaps I could shower and then wash my clothes?" she suggested.

"Make yourself at home." He reached into a closet, pulled out a black robe and handed it to her.

Trisha took it and held it close as if she were holding a part of him as he walked away. She followed him as far as the bedroom door then watched as he continued along the short, wood paneled hallway to the main part of the house. Coming or going she had to admit the man was impressive. She held the robe up to her face, surreptitiously inhaling the residual scent of his body, his soap and cologne in the fabric.

Oh, joy! What a way to start her day. Waking up in his bed on the tail end of a nightmare, now about to get naked and shower, drown herself in his robe, and then wash her clothes. How domestic was that?

She didn't care about him seeing her soiled shirt and jeans. But her underwear? Did she really want him to see the burgundy satin thong and the matching lace bra that she didn't need to wear? Was she going to risk the intimacy of her bare skin snuggling under the cozy fabric of his robe?

It came down to that or clean clothes. Sniffing suspiciously at her shirt she made a quick decision. He could show her where the washer and dryer were and she'd do everything herself. No need for him to see anything.

She marched into the bathroom and quickly stripped off, showered and washed her hair with a lemon-scented shampoo, then shrugged into the robe which enveloped her. Its hem pooled on the floor about her feet. Wry amusement bubbled up inside her when she caught sight of herself in the mirror and a reluctant chuckle escaped from her lips.

"Want to share the joke?" Cameron's voice drifted through the bathroom door.

Trisha folded the robe around her body and tied the sash firmly around her waist to prevent any bare skin from showing. From the looks he'd sent her way he might be tempted to unwrap her like a Christmas present. She bundled up her laundry and opened the door.

"I look like one of the seven dwarfs." She indicated the fabric dragging on the floor.

"None of them ever looked that good." Cameron grinned appreciatively at her. "Here, I'll take those for you."

Trisha hung on to the bundle of clothes and refused his offer. "No, you've been kind enough as it is. Just show me the way to the washer."

"Right this way, ma'am."

The twinkle in his eyes set Trisha's heart thumping. Would he still be as kind if her last nerve unraveled and she told him what she had done? She trailed him across the kitchen and through the door at the back of it.

"This is the garage, but the utility room's right here."

Trisha looked around in amazement at the expanse of floor and the high ceiling. "This isn't a garage, it's a parking lot."

Cameron laughed. "I do most of my own vehicle maintenance, so I need some place to do it. This is it. Here, let me show you the programs."

The sight of the space-age appliances arrayed against the wall made her take a second look.

"Where did you win the price of these?" The question came out of her mouth before she could stop it. She hoped he didn't think her rude.

He pursed his lips thoughtfully as he considered her query. "Las Vegas two years ago. I brought them back in the trailer tucked in beside Anchorman and a couple of other horses."

"Who looks after things for you when you're away?"

"That would be my neighbor, George. If you hang around here long enough you'll get to meet him."

With Cameron's help she selected a cold water wash for a small load and quickly placed her clothes in the machine.

"That's about a twenty minute wash," he told her. "Plenty of time for coffee and breakfast too, if you want anything to eat."

"I should phone Samantha first." Guilt that she'd been enjoying Cameron's tempting company far too much crept into her consciousness. She would have to be careful. "She'll probably be worrying where I am." Trisha paused and for a moment looked puzzled. "Um, where exactly am I?"

Cameron chuckled. "Just tell her you're with me at Coyle Creek. The phone's in my office there, off the hallway."

Trisha hadn't noticed the cunningly fitted pocket door before, but now slid it open and stepped inside. Western art and framed photographs of Cameron on and off horses, in mid-flight between horse and steer and behind the wheel of a tractor, hung on the walls. Floor to ceiling shelves were stacked with books and neatly labeled organizer boxes. The desk top sported piles of paperwork, a double banker's lamp, a large calendar pad with a pen beside it and the phone. Moving behind the desk she sank into a deep leather chair before realizing she didn't have Samantha's number.

Cameron followed her to the office, his large frame filling the doorway.

"You might need this." He handed her Samantha's business card.

Trisha took it and turned it in her fingers. "You must have read my mind."

She said thank you and smiled at him but his awareness disconcerted her. If he could determine her need for a telephone number so easily, what else might he pick up on? Not really comfortable with that possibility but intrigued by it, she reached for the phone.

She knew Samantha would probably rage indignantly at being abandoned but Trisha put the call through anyway. Before she could say more than hello, Samantha wanted to know exactly what had happened but then became blatant in her admonishments to steer clear of cowboys, especially the good looking variety.

"And don't let him kiss you."

Did the kiss Cameron dropped on her head yesterday, the one that could have been a dream, count? Probably not, at least not in the way Samantha meant. She laughed as she hung up and returned to the kitchen.

"Apparently I have to be back in town this evening for Sneak-a-Peek, whatever that is."

"That's the opening night of Stampede." Cameron juggled pans on the stove top then slid a plate of bacon, scrambled eggs and pancakes across the island for her. "The midway's open if you like rides and side shows and don't even think about calories when you get a bag of deep fried mini-donuts."

"Sounds like fun." Trisha sprinkled fresh ground pepper on her eggs and helped herself to ketchup. "I imagine it will be noisy."

"Uh-huh. Can be." Cameron sat down beside her. "The Parade is on Friday morning and then the show really gets going with the rodeo in the afternoon."

"That means you'll be busy."

Did he detect a wistful tone in her voice? He slid a sideways glance her way, but she avoided his eyes and concentrated on the food on her plate.

"Only during the day. Once the rodeo's over, my evenings are usually free and if I'm lucky I'll get a by-day. We could come out here if you'd like to go riding again."

"What's a by-day?"

Disappointed at the slick way she'd avoided his invitation, Cameron stifled a sigh. What was he thinking anyway? She was here for a few days and then would go back to her life in London, or wherever she lived. He cleared his throat.

"It means I've scored enough points that I can miss a go-round without penalty."

A loud buzzing sound indicated the end of the wash cycle and Cameron slid off his stool and left the kitchen.

Trisha almost choked on the fluffiest scrambled eggs she'd ever tasted, threw down her fork and grabbed the voluminous folds of Cameron's robe up around her ankles. She scurried after him but was too late to stop him placing her underwear in the dryer. Her cheeks burned as she saw the grin on his face.

"I could have done that," she insisted.

"My pleasure." Cameron's wicked grin widened. "I mean, it really is my pleasure. It'll all be dry in no time."

Trisha lifted her chin and spun around to return to the kitchen. She caught her heel on the hem of the robe and stumbled, swearing under her breath when she heard him chuckle. Back in the kitchen she hitched herself up on her stool and finished her breakfast, her mind tumbling as fast as the drier. She must be in the middle of a dream. Most men she knew were as transient as herself, not owning a stick of anything, knowing the way to the closest launderette like the backs of their hands and eating at pubs and greasy spoons. This man built his own house, did laundry and cooked. Why did he take so much pride in that?

Apart from the steak she'd had last night, she couldn't remember the last time she'd actually enjoyed her food so took her time eating her meal, savoring every mouthful.

"Where did you learn to make eggs like this?"

"Mom," he said. "She was a great cook."

Trisha sipped on her coffee. "Was?"

Cameron let out a long sigh. The pain in that sigh hit her and she wished she'd not asked.

"Ten years ago mom and dad took a trip to Reno. First vacation they'd had since they got married. It'd been a long time since Dad had driven any distance. We're not sure, but it's likely he fell asleep at the wheel. They hit the ditch and that was it."

"I'm so sorry." Instinctively wanting to empathize with him, Trisha reached out and covered his hand with her own. She understood only too well that accidents happened. "That must have been hard. But you said 'we'. You have siblings?"

Cameron turned his hand over and without looking at her gripped fingers and rubbed his thumb over her knuckles. "A younger brother, Mackenzie."

The thinning of his lips told their own story. No doubt there that bad blood existed between them. She should leave it alone but her curiosity got the better of her. "You don't get on with him?"

"You could say that."

Another buzzer sounded and a boyish grin swept away anything else he might have said. "That's for you. Your clothes should be dry."

"I'll get them, thank you all the same." Head high, Trisha once more gathered up the robe and went to retrieve her clothes.

* * *

"So?" Samantha waggled her eyebrows suggestively as Trisha walked into the office.

"So what?" Trisha shrugged a shoulder. "You were the one who told me to steer clear of good looking cowboys and not let them kiss me so there's nothing to tell."

"Oh, no, you're not getting off that lightly." Samantha cuffed the shoulder Trisha so carelessly shrugged. "You disappear on me with that gorgeous sample of manhood, spend the night with him in some remote location and give me a 'so what'? That tells me you're trying to shut the stable door after the horse has bolted. Not good enough, my friend. I need to live vicariously. Try again."

Trisha sat down in one of the chairs by Samantha's desk and tipped her head back. "Went horseback riding. Saw a cougar. Cameron took me to supper and dancing, then I went to sleep and he put me to bed. Woke up. Showered, had breakfast while my clothes were in the washer ..."

"Hah!" Samantha pointed a French manicured finger at her. "So you were naked."

"Beneath the robe he provided me with, yes."

"That's it?" Samantha sounded aggrieved. "When are you seeing him again?"

Trisha hesitated. She hadn't wanted to part from Cameron at all. He'd lifted her down from his truck in the alley out back of Samantha's office block and held her so long she was sure he was going to kiss her. But then an impatient delivery truck driver honked his horn because Cameron's Ford blocked his way. Cameron waved at the driver to wait, fished a cell phone out of his dashboard cubby and handed it to her.

"This is my back up phone. My number's the only number listed on it," he'd said. "Call me. We'll go out Saturday night."

The hard shape of the phone in her jeans pocket pressed against her thigh. Her heart lightened. He wanted to be sure she could contact him and must have assumed she didn't have a phone. She looked for the bag containing her own phone, her passport, lip gloss and other essentials dumped two days ago. She retrieved it with relief then looked at Samantha.

"Saturday," she said. "Unless there's anything else we have to do or place we have to be."

"Ah, yes," Samantha began. "Actually, I meant to have a word with you."

Trisha didn't like the silence that followed Samantha's hesitant utterance.

"Samantha, what have you done?"

"Well, you were coming to Calgary anyway." Samantha played with a pen on her desk and avoided Trisha's eyes. "And you're a damn good photographer. Who better than you to put faces with photos and talk about the best qualities you see in them? So I sort of told my client you'd introduce the models for her publishing house's book cover competition at their gala evening."

"You did what?" Trisha glared at Samantha. "How could you? You said you wanted me to help pick photos for your agency, and now you want me to help host a gala evening?"

"I know, sweetie, I know, but it really won't take up much of your time. There's a reception dinner on Friday night at the Palliser

Hotel. Anyway, you'd be taking time to eat somewhere for goodness sake, and you can't deny that I promised you lots of hot cowboys."

Trisha shook her head in disbelief. "I really cannot believe you did that. Talk about dropping me in the deep end. And what's this competition for again?"

"Purple Plain publishes western romance novels and they're looking for new cover models. Sorry, I didn't think you'd mind too much." Samantha shrugged her shoulders and didn't look at all sorry. "And you do owe me a favor for introducing you as the best new photog on the block to that big shot Hollywood actor. Didn't you get an invite to visit with him and his family at their private lake property in Quebec?"

On a very deep level Trisha had somehow known that favor would come back at her one day. She caught her bottom lip between her teeth. The introduction had netted a feature for a classy international news magazine and a yet-to-be-acted upon invitation to visit the celeb family ranch in Montana. "So what exactly have you told your client I will do?"

"The photographs will be set up on easels on the stage—"

"Stage?" Trisha leaped to her feet and strode around Samantha's office wishing she could hit something.

"Sweetie, I told you this is at the Palliser, one of the best and certainly the oldest hotel in town. It's a big deal for the publishing house. All you have to do is uncover a portrait and then call that contestant on the stage until the line-up is complete. They're all of them yummy, I promise you."

"Good Lord." Trisha smacked her hand against her head. "I should have stayed at the YWCA. Life would have been far simpler."

"Simpler maybe, but not as much fun, and you my dear English friend, could definitely do with a dose of that."

Defeated, Trisha stumbled into the nearest chair. "So what do I need to wear for this bash?"

"Western wear is good," Samantha said. "But if you want to knock 'em dead wear a dress and killer heels."

"Like black lace and Louboutin's?" Trisha asked sarcastically.

"Just like that," Samantha agreed.

Trisha gave her a scathing glance. "Yeah, those I pack with me everywhere I go."

Samantha grinned and lifted her eyebrows. "You forget to whom you are talking. I will be your fairy godmother and you shall go to the ball, but now we're going home for me to change and then we're going to Sneak-a-Peek."

Chapter Six

As they strolled through the Stampede Grounds, Samantha explained how cowboy Guy Weadick had started the whole show more than a century ago. Trisha half heard the narrative but couldn't help thinking about Cameron and how right he'd been about the mini-donuts. The bag containing them, fresh from the fryer, warmed her hand just as thinking about him warmed her heart.

She had to stop that and concentrated instead on steeling herself against the bright lights and the noise around them. Being part of such a large crowd at first set her nerves on edge, but then the sheer novelty of it all lightened her mood.

She nibbled on another mini-donut, still listening to Samantha but thinking more of Cameron. It was no surprise to her that when she looked up, there he stood. Her hand itched to slip into his, but Samantha would surely notice and prompt a conversation Trisha didn't want to have.

"Hello ladies." Cameron tipped his hat.

"Well, Mr. Carter, how nice to see you." Samantha batted her eyelashes at him. Her suspiciously bright smile failed to screen the anything-but-innocent look she slid over him to Trisha and back again. "Could I persuade you to look after my guest for a while? I've just spotted someone that I absolutely have to speak to."

Samantha melted into the crowd, leaving Trisha and Cameron looking at each other. Momentarily speechless, Trisha took a deep breath and then slid her hand into his. Cameron lifted it and kissed the back of her fingers.

"I'm glad you did that."

"I am too." Trisha licked her suddenly dry lips, not trusting herself to say more, shocked at herself for having taken the initiative but she so wanted to touch him.

"Have you been around the sideshows yet?" Cameron placed his arm loosely around her and tugged her to his side.

She could have shrugged his arm off but she didn't want to and snuggled closer to him instead, letting herself believe just for a moment that they were like any other couple enjoying the evening. They wandered along the rows of amusement kiosks, jostled with other people enjoying a night amid the lights and bustle of the fair grounds.

Trisha's nose twitched at the pungent aromas of deep fryers serving up chicken wings and other things she couldn't believe people would even think of eating. Cameron's arm dropped from her shoulders as he stopped to talk to a vendor serving up beef on a bun. Jostled by the crowd, Trisha found herself separated from him and tried to push her way back to his side.

Then a sound as sharp as the crack of Cameron's rifle burst in her ears.

Nausea churned her stomach, her chest tightened and she panicked. She clapped her hands over her ears and ran for the shelter of the nearest kiosk, trembling like a frightened animal.

Cameron saw her and pushed people out of his way in his hurry to get to her. He crouched beside her, alarmed at the tremors that convulsed her. Heat still radiated off the pavement but he could hear her teeth chattering. She lifted her head and he saw with dismay her wide, sightless eyes.

"Don't let it happen," she hissed at him. "Please don't let it happen."

"Honey, it's just the fireworks." Cameron gently reached for her and drew her into his arms. She turned her face into his chest and he felt every shiver and sob that wracked her body.

The kiosk operator looked at them curiously. "Everything all right there?"

Cameron nodded but when a rocket burst in a shower of red and green lights above their heads, Trisha went limp.

"Damn." As Cameron scooped her into his arms he couldn't imagine what caused her to be this fearful of loud sounds. It had to have been something truly horrific.

"She had too much to drink?" The kiosk operator eyed them both with suspicion.

Cameron shook his head. "Where's the closest first aid station?"

"In the Big Four Building."

"Thanks." Cameron picked up Trisha with ease and made his way through the crowds which quickly parted for him as they sensed some emergency. He'd almost made it to the Big Four entrance doors when Trisha whispered, "Why are you carrying me?"

"You passed out again. I'm taking you to the first aid station."

"No. Please don't." Trisha wound her arms around his neck and clung tight. "I'm fine. Really."

Cameron stopped, carefully set her down on her feet but held her against him. She'd insisted she was fine once before and nearly passed out again. He wasn't taking any chances now. He examined her face, noticed how pale she was, saw the fatigue in her eyes and realized how exhausted she must be.

"I'm taking you home," he said. "Think you can walk back to my truck?"

She nodded and he slipped his arm around her waist. They didn't speak during the long hike back to the parking lot.

His mind raced. Loud noises didn't just startle her but scared the bejesus out of her. Had she been mugged? Had she been in an accident? Was that it? When they reached his truck he simply lifted her up into it. She was still shivering and he pulled out the blanket from its place behind the seat and wrapped it around her.

"Trisha ..." he began.

"No." She covered her face with her hands. "I don't want to talk about it."

Cameron glanced at her as he slid into his seat but she had already turned away from him and drawn the blanket up over her face.

"Where does Samantha live?" he asked.

"Downtown, by the river," came the muffled reply. "I don't know the exact address, but I'll know it when we get there. It's off Third Avenue and Eighth Street."

Cameron eased into the flow of traffic. It hardly moved, but he hoped the delay might give Trisha time to recover herself.

Light blazed from bars and restaurants, illuminating the crowds of people congregating on the darkened sidewalks. The traffic continued to move at a snail's pace, both sides of the street packed with a long line of vehicles. Laughter and a fair amount of hooting and hollering punctuated the hum of idling motors as the traffic backed up between sets of lights.

The slow drive gave him time to think. How could he get Trisha to talk about what had happened to her? That it was something serious he had no doubt. Her reaction to loud noises and bright lights, the scar on her forehead all indicated something that went deep and was way outside his experience. He braked and turned a corner.

"Trisha, you need to give me directions from here." He reached out and gently shook her shoulder.

The blanket whispered softly against her cheek as she pushed it back, the seat belt creaked as she sat up. He glanced sideways at her and saw her adjust her hat and carefully finger the fall of hair over the right side of her face.

"Okay. This is Samantha's building." She pointed to a new-looking condo block.

Cameron parked at the curb but by the time he reached the passenger door she already stood on the sidewalk.

"There's no need to walk me to the door. It's right there." She indicated the building's front entrance.

"There's every need." He took her arm, leaving her no time to argue. "This is downtown Calgary, past midnight and Stampede has just started. You have no idea who might be about, what state they might be in or what they might do. Don't argue."

Trisha snapped her mouth shut. Who did he think he was, just taking charge like that? She'd managed on her own for longer than she wanted to admit. Her spark of annoyance quickly faded as she thought of all the kindness he'd shown her. If she were honest, she couldn't deny the comfort in just letting him take over and relying on him for just a smidgeon of time. They reached the main doors, all sparkling glass and gleaming brass, the whole area bathed in light and observed by security cameras. Trisha keyed Samantha's security code in on the entrance panel. They listened to it ring but no one answered.

"Do you need my phone?" Cameron asked.

"No, thank you." She pulled out her own phone from her jeans pocket and thumbed a speed dial number, listening for a moment to the ring tone. When she didn't get an answer, she quickly keyed in a text message. They waited in silence for a response, but none came. "Well, I guess if all else fails I'll get a hotel for the night."

"First night of Stampede?" Cameron shook his head. "Forget it. Everything even half way decent will have been booked for months in advance and anything else is no place for you. Come on."

"Where are we going?"

"My brother's house."

"Will he mind?"

Cameron snorted with something like derision. "He's never there. Mackenzie heads security for a diamond cutting company in Mauritius. He won't be here until Christmas or New Year, if at all. I deal with the real estate agent who sets up corporate rentals for him. It's between tenants right now and it's empty."

He boosted her into the truck and again they were driving, this time crossing the river.

Trisha lost all sense of direction as Cameron negotiated intersections and bends in the road, but then he turned on to a driveway, hit a remote on his visor and drove into the garage that opened up in front of them. She listened to the light clank of the overhead door closing and caught her breath. Here she was again, in a strange location with a man she now knew only slightly better than two days ago.

Was it really only two days? It was more like years. That she had known him forever. That he had always been in her life instead of appearing in it just a short while ago. She slid out of the truck.

Cameron turned on a light and unlocked a door which Trisha supposed must lead into the house. "This way. I'll show you to the guest room."

She followed him through the doorway, fixing her eyes on his broad back and reining in the urge to run her hands over the curves of his butt. She'd forgotten that all consuming hot, hungry sensation of wanting someone, of needing their touch so much her body ached. That hunger raced through her now but hotter, more demanding. She wanted him. Needed him so much it almost blinded her.

He turned to her as they reached the stairs and caught his breath at the sight of her face, pale but for the high, bright spots of color in her cheeks. Her eyes were wide and suspiciously bright, her lips slightly parted and moist as if she'd just licked them. If she hadn't then hell, he'd lick them for her. He stopped so abruptly she almost walked in to him.

"Trisha, have you any idea what your eyes are saying to me?" he asked softly.

She shook her head.

"You're looking at me like you want to eat me alive." Cameron took a step closer to her.

"What if I do?" Guilt and anticipation swirled in her mind. Suddenly tired of the burden she carried, she allowed anticipation to push the guilt aside. Heat surged in her veins as he took another step towards her.

"What if I can't say no?" Cameron watched the pink tip of her tongue sweep across her lower lip. He groaned inwardly. Did she have to do that right then? His pulse hiked up a notch.

She looked up at his taut features, the skin stretched across his cheek bones and jaws, his nostrils pinched as if holding his breath. Reaching up she touched the flat plane of his cheek with her fingertips.

"What if I don't want you to?"

The barely stifled groan she'd heard moments ago now rumbled deep in his throat and for a moment Trisha was afraid he would turn away from her. But then he hooked a finger into her belt and gently pulled her up against his body.

"If you want to say 'No', now is the time to do it," he whispered, "because if I kiss you properly, the way I want to, with my tongue deep in your throat, I will not be able to stop."

She saw the glitter of arousal in his eyes, the evidence of it hard in his jeans where her belly butted against his. Her own arousal signaled itself with a rush of heat between her legs.

She closed her eyes as she raised her face for his kiss. His lips were full and soft, light as a dream but she sensed the weight of wanting in them and opened her mouth, inhaling with sheer delight as his tongue slid against hers. She couldn't think, didn't want to think. Only wanted to give in to the sensations that raced through her, to feel again emotions suppressed for far too long. She teased Cameron's tongue, exploring its soft underside with her own, relished the heat and shape of his mouth and taste of his lips.

She hooked her leg around his to hold him closer, gave in to her own increasing demands and strained against him. Cameron grasped her buttocks and lifted her up.

"Do you want it hard and fast or slow and easy?" His whisper flowed as sweet as molten honey across her neck.

Sliding her other leg around him she gripped him tightly, balancing her core against his centre. The pounding threat of her climax tightened the muscles in her lower belly.

"Hard." She gripped him more tightly.

Cameron took a step and boosted her up against the wall. Held in place with a firm surface at her back and the hot reality of his erection between her legs, she cried out as Cameron dipped his head and swept his tongue up the long line of her throat.

"Come for me, sweetheart," he whispered. "Just let go."

She moaned and bucked against him while his firm but gentle fingers kneaded the soft curves of her buttocks. Each time he squeezed she pushed hard against him.

"That's it, Trish, let me have it." He held her to him, grinding his body against hers until her moan became a gasp.

She arched against him and threw her head back. It hit the wall with a bang as she convulsed against his erection and a cry of delight burst from her throat. Even with the fabric of their jeans between them Cameron felt her unexpectedly strong climax as it rippled through her.

He closed his eyes as he buried his face into her shoulder. For a moment he just held her, adjusting his furious breathing with hers. Gradually she relaxed and he lifted his head and looked at her. Was this the same girl? Her eyes were closed and her lashes fanned across her pink-flushed cheeks. A smile hovered on her lips. Then she opened her eyes and looked into his.

"That wasn't enough, Cameron. Please take me to bed." She dropped her head onto his shoulder and pressed her lips against his neck. She nibbled at his ear lobe and used her tongue in a way that made him forget his name.

The ache in his jeans was not going to go away, and she had asked him to take her to bed. She'd even said please. His momma raised him to always help a lady, so he did just that.

Chapter Seven

Cameron carried her upstairs with no effort at all. He nudged open a door with his shoulder. In the dim light filtering through the window, Trisha could make out the outline of the bed and sighed with pleasure as Cameron laid her on it.

"You're very good at putting me to bed." Her voice quivered a little with a hint of laughter.

"I'm glad you think so." Cameron sank down beside her and grinned as she turned to him and pressed her body against his. He started to stroke her hair back from her face but she caught his wrist.

"Not that," she whispered against his chest.

Her sudden stillness caused him to pause, but he caught her fingers and kissed them.

"All right, not that," he agreed. He remembered the scar her hair screened, wanted to know the cause of it but knew that question would have to wait.

She relaxed into him and wound her arms around his waist, lifted her face for the kiss he was more than happy to oblige her with. His heart pounded painfully in his chest as his lips covered hers. Blood rushed in his ears as he pulled her closer. Her frantic fingers tugged at his shirt and pulled the fabric free from the restraint of his waistband. Cool air flowed across his skin like a whisper as she pushed his shirt aside.

Her lips trailed across his stomach, followed by the wet heat of her tongue as she slowly swept it across his bare chest. His nipples tightened as she circled one, then the other with a slow, teasing finger tip. She straddled him and continued to trace the outline of his chest muscles with her fingernails. He closed his eyes when she leaned over him, her hair falling forward on his face. Then she kissed him, her ravenous mouth every bit as demanding as his had been.

His hands swept up into her hair and he cradled the back of her head, meeting her tongue with a wildness that made him forget the world outside the window, forget everything except the woman he held here and now in his arms. But holding her wasn't enough. He wanted to see her, to kiss every inch of her, to be inside her. He rolled her onto her back and started to unbutton her shirt with trembling fingers.

Hell. What was wrong with him? He'd never had trouble getting a woman's shirt off before but suddenly his fingers were fat and ungainly and he fumbled each button until they were all undone. Trisha didn't seem to notice his ineptness as she worked at undoing his buttons. Both shirts were now gone, thrown beyond the bed.

Cameron drew back slightly and looked down at her. She was as perfect as he'd imagined she would be. He ran his hand up the smoothness of her long, lean body and palmed one of her perfect breasts. The sigh that drifted from her made him smile.

"I've wanted to do this since I first set eyes on you."

The yearning in his voice reached somewhere deep inside her. Now was not the time for words, talking could come later. She pushed herself up into his hand, wordlessly telling him how much she craved his touch.

He dropped his head to her breast and drew its rosy peak into the warmth of his mouth. An explosion of sensations coursed through her, one following fast on the tail of another, giving her no time to savor each delightful discovery. She wound her arms around his head and held him as close to her as she could. Her nipple puckered even more when he released it, the air cooling it and making it fold in on itself into a hard little bud.

"Noo-oo, Cameron, don't stop." A moan followed by a sigh of pleasure escaped her lips as he suckled her other nipple. She raked her fingers through his hair and kissed whatever patch of skin she could reach until he lifted his head from her breast. Cradling his face in her hands she looked into the storm-cloud grey of his eyes and saw the wanting in them. Unable to resist, she drew him down to her, opening her mouth under his, taking his tongue as eagerly as she wanted to take the rest of him.

Her body burnt with the scorching certainty that there was only one way to quench her inner fire. She wanted him, all of him, but when she placed her hand on him, he shuddered and lay still.

She smiled as she sensed the reason. "You nearly came, didn't you?"

Breathing hard Cameron turned on to his back. "Just like a damn teenager at his first go-round."

Trisha buried her face in the soft hair on his chest and giggled. Cameron closed his eyes and groaned as her fingers reached for his waistband.

"Breath in," she ordered. He sucked in his breath as she slid his zipper open, easing it over his impressive erection. She tugged his jeans down over his hips, pulled them down his legs and tossed them on the floor. "Lift up."

His boxers followed and Trisha sat back on her heels, her eyes wide as she saw him for the first time.

"Oh, my."

The pure pleasure in her voice made Cameron open his eyes. The surprise and awe he saw in her expression filled him with satisfaction, but he closed his eyes again with a sigh as her hand tightened around him. Whatever else happened tonight, he was a goner in more ways than one.

A heightened awareness flooded Trisha's belly as she tightened her fist around him. She leaned down and ran her tongue down the length of him, swirled it around the rough ridges of his tightly drawn testicles, breathed in the salty scent of him. Cameron shot up on the bed.

"Don't you like that?" Trisha asked, surprised at his reaction.

"Are you kidding?" Cameron drew her into his arms. What could he say? He wanted to tell her how she'd thrown him for a loop, captured his heart with that first green-eyed glance. Nope, Carter, she won't fall for that. Try the truth. "You've got your hands and tongue all over me, sweetheart. What's not to like?"

He heard her contented sigh as he pulled her closer, kissing her slowly, thoroughly, teasing his tongue at the corner of her mouth, sliding it over the fullness of her bottom lip and tasting her all over again. Then he suddenly lifted his head and looked down the length of her body.

"But there is something wrong with this picture."

A sudden chill ran through her. What had she done or not done? Did he regret bringing her here and being with her? She stiffened with apprehension.

"What do you mean?"

The wariness in her expression caught him off guard but he grinned at her and dropped a swift kiss on her mouth. "One of us is still wearing clothes."

Trisha instantly twisted away from him, hoping he wouldn't see the relief she was sure must show on her face. He caught her, pulled her back and reached for her waistband. He popped the button and lowered the zipper enough to reveal the flat plain of her belly and trailed his finger over her smooth-as-satin skin, watching the rippling tremors his touch produced. He listened to the catch in her breath before opening the zipper the rest of the way, revealing a black satin and red lace thong.

"You sure like your fancy underwear," he said.

The light in his eyes warmed her to her core and she relished the sensation of the denim sliding down her legs as he slowly peeled off her jeans. She shivered as he placed his hands on her hips and spread his fingers across her belly then hooked his thumbs under the edges of her thong.

Her skin pebbled with anticipation as his thumbs prescribed slow circles moving closer and closer to her already engorged centre. Her breathing shortened and she pushed up against his hands but he moved them away and shifted down the bed. The moan of dismay that formed in her throat turned into a gasp of delight as Cameron's hot mouth covered her mound.

He suckled her through the satin scrap that covered her, his hands now under her buttocks lifting her as though she was a juicy morsel for him to feast upon. He sensed her tension building as she strained against his mouth. The muscles along the inside of her thighs quivered and he stopped before she reached her climax.

He tugged the scrap of fabric off her and smiled down at her.

"Perfect," he whispered.

It might not be in his bed but here she was, just where he'd wanted her to be from the moment he'd first set eyes on her. Naked and beneath him.

She reached up for him. Cameron gathered her into his arms and buried his face in her neck. She held him with a strength and urgency he had not expected. It hinted of desperation, as if she might expect him to cut and run. If she'd only trust him with her fears he might be able to quell them. But now was not the time for whispered reassurances. Now was the time to put out the fire she'd started in his body and his brain.

He kissed her chin, slid his hungry mouth to her neck and nearly came undone as she opened her legs for him. He reached out blindly for his jeans until his fingers gripped his wallet. He pulled out a square foil packet and ripped it open with his teeth. Trisha took it from him.

"Cameron, I can't wait much longer," she pleaded as she rolled the latex over him.

"You won't have to," he assured her.

He pushed against her hot, wet, swollen lips and slowly slid inside her. Man, she was tight. Every muscle in his body screamed at him to let go, every instinct willed him to drive home. But he caught and held himself, floundering in a trough between the pain of a fierce hard-on and the pleasure of what was to follow.

"Now I know what it must be like to give birth." He braced himself on his arms and dropped his forehead to rest on hers.

Trisha looked up at him, wide-eyed with surprise. "What?"

"The need to push," he groaned.

The laugh that rolled through Trisha released the remaining tension in her muscles. Cameron closed his eyes as he moved further into her. If there was heaven on earth, this was it.

Her inner muscles gripped him like a velvet vise. His breath hitched painfully in his throat when she tightened her muscles even more in short, quick pulses of pressure. When she softened her grip, he let out his breath in a slow exhale and sank all the way into her.

She wrapped her long legs around him and moved with him, matched every one of his strokes with one of her own. Her arms wound around his back and held him close. Her lips moved on his neck murmuring words that didn't reach his ears but her notes of passion were as clear as if she'd sung them. Her breath on his skin was a pleasure so strong, so sinfully intense it blurred his vision.

But then she arched her back and her body strained against his, each supple movement urging him on. Her cries filled the heated air around them and he drew in a sharp breath as her nails dug into the skin on his back.

It was the only spur he needed. He drove into her again and again and roared his release as Trisha screamed hers.

* * *

Cameron lay on his back, one arm thrown across his face and Trisha curled up in the crook of the other. The fact that she was the only woman to go to bed with him and still be there in the morning was not lost on him. He drew her closer, knowing that what they'd shared wasn't just sex, that it had been a melding of every possible element between them.

It scared the hell out of him, as did the fact that he didn't want to let her go.

She shifted and looked up at him. Her heart had slowed to its regular steady beat but now turned cold. Even though his arm had tightened around her, couldn't he even look at her? She sensed they had experienced something monumental, but how long lasting could that be if he learnt the truth about her? She sat up and shifted to the side of the bed.

Cameron caught her wrist. "Where are you going?"

"To the bathroom."

He let her go. Her feet made no sound as she crossed the deep pile carpet. She walked into the en-suite and closed the door before fumbling for the switch and turning on the light.

Catching sight of herself in the mirror, she gasped in dismay. Her hair, messed up and tumbled every which way, hung over her flushed cheeks. Her lips were still swollen from Cameron's kisses, kisses she had been only too willing to return.

Tears filled her eyes. How could she have done this? How could she have so easily used him to salve her conscience? He deserved better. And how could she get out of this without her heart breaking all over again but for very different reasons?

Chapter Eight

He'd fallen asleep, his breathing deep and even. Uncertainty made Trisha hover beside the bed. Should she crawl back in beside him, leave him or wake him up? Making that decision was taken from her when he flung out an arm, obviously searching for her. His eyes flew open and he sat up in apparent alarm at not finding her beside him.

Trisha half smiled at the realization he still wanted her and slid under the covers.

"It's so warm here," she whispered as she nestled into his arms.

"Could be warmer still." He turned on his side, taking her with him as he nuzzled her neck and ran a hand down her bare back.

Her eyelids drifted shut in dreamy delight as Cameron's fingers made lazy circles at the base of her spine. His thumbs slid over her hip bones and whisked over her thigh until his hand nestled behind her knee. Lifting her leg over his waist made it easy for Trisha to take his rampant length into her with a sigh.

What previously had been raw, hard sex became slow, gentle loving. Fingers touched, tangled, explored. Soft, sweet kisses mingled with satisfied sighs and moans of delight. Trisha's body came alive, tingling from head to toe under Cameron's touch. His breath whispered over her skin making her shiver with need. He was all hard muscle under her hands yet she marveled how her touch caused him to tremble.

They rode each other with measured strokes until their pleasure grew, spiked until their breathing shortened in quick sharp gasps. They needed no words for one to encourage the other to move faster, harder, to be guided by the urgency in their sweat slicked bodies. Their climax came in a rush of heat, of quivering muscles and blinding light, of pleasure so deep and extraordinary it bordered on pain.

They held on to each other, riding the quivering aftermath of their lovemaking, their hearts beating in unison while they inhaled each other's breath and waited for the sensations still shaking them to subside.

Cameron's breath still rasped in and out of his chest with exertion as Trisha turned her face into the pillow. What they shared was so far beyond anything she had ever experienced and she did not want to consider the implications of what that might mean. Before she could even begin to think of what to say, Cameron groaned. She lifted her head and was shocked to see a broad swath of sunlight splashed across the bedroom wall.

"Morning? Already?"

"Yup." Cameron rolled out of bed and headed to the bathroom.

Trisha peered at her watch and read four-thirty a.m. It was her turn to groan. Where had the night gone? After a very short shower Cameron returned to the bedroom with one towel slung around his hips, another over his head as he vigorously rubbed his hair dry.

"I've got to get down to the grounds." The towel muffled his voice but then he pulled it aside and grinned at her. "Do you want to come with me?"

"I believe I already did."

Cameron threw the damp towel at her. Trisha laughed even though the thought of him leaving made her heart heavy. "If you don't mind, I think I'll stay here and get a cab over to Samantha's a bit later. Can I make you coffee?"

"I'd love it, but there's no time now." Cameron pulled on his jeans. "Everything you need's in the kitchen, so just make yourself at home."

"What if your brother walks in?"

Cameron straightened up and reached for his shirt. "Not likely. But if he does, you're a Stampede tenant."

Trisha absorbed that information and while Cameron finished dressing, grabbed a towel and wrapped herself in it. She made her way downstairs to the kitchen. The expanse of granite counter tops and stainless steel appliances reminded her of Cameron's kitchen. The two brothers' tastes in décor were remarkably similar.

Cameron came downstairs in a rush, shoved his feet into his boots and grabbed his hat. He couldn't believe his awkwardness. He'd shared something deep and precious with Trisha and leaving her was the last thing he wanted to do.

He couldn't think of a darn thing to say to her as he stopped at the door with one hand about to turn the knob, the other on his hip, his gaze on the floor.

Hell, talk about a tongue-tied teenager. He didn't want her to think that last night was all he'd wanted from her. Nothing could be further than the truth but he couldn't make her any promises. Not until he knew for sure exactly what he did want.

He had to go but every part of him wanted to stay. He dared to look back at her and wished he hadn't. She stood by the kitchen counter, clutching the towel around her slim body. Her un-brushed hair curtained her face but not enough to prevent him seeing a suspicious sheen forming in her eyes.

What was with that? He'd given her fair warning of what to expect, knowing he'd find it hard to hold back. Had his lovemaking been too much for her? Or did she think he'd got what he'd wanted and was walking out on her? He didn't have time to ask or to reassure her, he knew he was running late and had to get moving.

"Oh, damn," he said softly as he went back to her. "Don't cry, sweetheart. I didn't hurt you, did I?"

He whisked a tear from her cheek with his thumb then leaned in to kiss her.

"No, you didn't," she whispered when their lips parted. Reaching up she laid her hand on his cheek. "I'm being unreasonable. I just don't want you to go."

"I'm sorry, but I have to get my butt in gear." He took her hand and kissed her fingers, swore again and then tore himself away. "I'll call you later."

Trisha listened to the purr of the truck engine, the mechanical whirr of the overhead door as it opened and closed, then the silence once Cameron was gone. The emptiness engulfing her rocked her to her core.

She sniffed hard and swiped her hand across her face. How could she possibly feel so much for a man she so recently met and knew so little about? How had she allowed this to happen? The pain now would be nothing to what it would be if her past history became known. She couldn't let it ruin what had to be a short time together.

"Time to pull up your big girl panties," she told herself. She sniffed again and ignored the knot of tension forming in her stomach as she returned to the chaos of the bedroom. The comforter lay half on, half off the bed. Her clothes were strewn across the floor and she sighed as she started picking them up. If she spent any more time with Cameron she'd have to invest in a launderette. She shook out her jeans and shirt, laid them across the bed to smooth out the worst of the creases before taking a shower.

Once dry and dressed, she surveyed the crumpled bedding and piles of damp towels with some consternation. Cameron hadn't said he was coming back, and she didn't think there was any room-service to tidy up after them. She quickly straightened the sheets and comforter and arranged the towels over the edge of the bath and shower rail to air dry. When she had done what she could, she ran downstairs and let herself out of the house. The door swung closed behind her with a solid thunk, but she checked it all the same. Satisfied that it was secure, she walked down the driveway and crossed the road.

Despite the early hour the sun already blazed in a crystal-clear blue sky and the reflection off the acres of glass on the downtown buildings dazzled her. A few runners jogged past her, dog walkers wished her good morning, all while her heart and head warred with each other.

Far below the pathway on which she walked, the fast flowing river sparkled like a living thing. It separated her from Samantha's condo, but when she reached a point opposite the building, she stopped and pulled out her phone.

"'Lo? That you Trisha?" Samantha's voice sounded heavy with sleep but then she let out a screech. "Are you nuts? It's not even six. Where the hell are you?"

"Look out your window and I'll wave to you," Trisha said.

"What are you doing over the river in Crescent Heights?" Samantha sounded wide awake now. "Don't answer that, just stay there and give me a few minutes. I'll come and pick you up."

Trisha closed her phone and sat on the low balustrade separating the road from the path. She pushed her hands into her pockets and slumped down. She couldn't get Cameron out of her head and didn't want to. He'd annoyed her at first but that, she admitted, had been as much her fault as his. Now his kindness, his gentleness, his sense of humor made her want to believe in a future.

For a brief moment she allowed herself to imagine what being with Cameron would be like. She could think of nothing better than making a home together. But how could it possibly work? These thoughts had to stop. They would lead nowhere.

She wouldn't risk the crippling pain of loss all over again. No, she would see him as much as she could while she was here and then she'd walk away.

A sudden blast of music from the east end of town brought her out of her reverie, reminding her that today was Stampede Parade day. Maybe that was why Cameron had to leave so early. Was he riding in the Parade? He hadn't said so but then, anything was possible.

Trisha didn't hear the car pull up behind her, wasn't aware of anything or anyone until Samantha flopped down beside her.

"Penny for them," she said, nudging Trisha's shoulder.

Trisha turned to her, ignoring Samantha's questioning look and shocked gasp.

"Oh, my god, girl. I take it you had a good night?"

"Unforgettable," Trisha agreed in a voice not much above a whisper.

She dropped her gaze to avoid Samantha's piercing scrutiny but failed miserably. Samantha nudged her again and asked quietly, "You've fallen in love with him, haven't you?"

"What?" Trisha's breath hitched in her throat. "No, of course I haven't."

Another blast of music from downtown prevented Samantha from asking any more disconcerting questions. Trisha boosted herself off the rail, thankful for the interruption. How could she admit anything to Samantha that she was not first going to admit to herself?

"Come on," she said. "Don't we have to watch a parade or something?"

Samantha looked at her watch. "Not before we get you home for a fresh change of clothes. Your car awaits, my lady."

She did her best impression of an English accent, but her efforts went unnoticed as Trisha slid into the luxury of the car's navy suede upholstery. The lost look in her eyes worried Samantha as did the weight loss and her friend's dry, brittle manner. She appeared as fragile as a winter twig that would snap under the slightest pressure.

"You know," she offered as she stopped at traffic lights, "fantastic sex doesn't necessarily equal love."

"This was not just sex," Trisha insisted. "I don't even want to try and describe what it was. And don't you dare ask for details."

"Spoil sport," Samantha grumbled, but then relented. "Look, you've never been hip-deep in cowboys before. They are overwhelmingly rugged, strong, sexy men. You could meet another guy in ten minutes that would obliterate Cameron Carter forever."

"Nice try, Samantha, but you're wrong."

"Sweetie—"

"Don't say anything. Just don't." Trisha put up her hands as if fending off whatever Samantha intended saying. "You know I've dated, you know Tony and I had a long term relationship, but nothing like this has ever happened to me before."

"So what are you going to do about it?" Samantha drove into the gloom of her condo's underground parking lot.

"Do?" Trisha sighed with resignation and shook her head. "Nothing."

"Nothing?" Samantha pulled up in her stall and looked at Trisha in disbelief. "You're telling me you've never felt like this before, not even with that jerk Tony who you fortunately didn't marry and you're going to do nothing?"

"How could anything between us really work?" Trisha blurted. "Think about it Sammie, he's this side of the pond and I'm the other.

Whether I like it or not I travel, a lot. How'd we deal with that?" She rubbed her forehead wearily. "I'll help you with your cowboy photographs and the cover models then I'll complete my assignment and go home. End of story. Now I think it's time to go get ready to watch this parade you've been yakking on about."

"Oh, crap," Samantha muttered as Trisha, face pale and mouth a curt tight line, shot out of the car but then crumpled against it, dropping her head onto her folded arms on its roof. Samantha stood beside her and slipped an arm around her shoulders.

"I'm sorry I snapped at you," Trisha mumbled.

"I'm sorry I bugged you." Samantha gave her a squeeze. "We must be the sorriest pair on the block. Come on. We'll get changed and leave the car here. We can walk up Eighth Street and if we're lucky we'll find a spot to take in the parade."

Trisha agreed, too exhausted to argue. How she wished she'd never made that phone call to Samantha in the first place, or that she'd allowed herself to be jockeyed into Samantha's wretched schemes.

Most of all, and much too late, she wished she'd never loved that cowboy.

Chapter Nine

People crammed the sidewalks, shoulder to shoulder, for as far as Trisha could see. She doubted even a thin piece of paper could be wedged between them. Some spectators had settled themselves in lawn chairs or on camp stools and many of the children sitting on the curbs held flags ready to wave.

She listened to smatterings of several languages from French to Japanese, all high on expectancy and the thrill of the moment. Heat shimmered off the road surface and intensified between the walls of the high rise buildings on either side of the street.

The first group of riders came into sight and Trisha craned her neck along with the rest of the crowd in an effort to see them better. A car with a plaque on its side advertising the Parade Marshal drove slowly by, its occupants smiling and waving to the cheering crowds.

The noise level rose and fell in waves of sound. She tensed, knowing what the shock of it could do but fought to control her breathing and braced herself. But the vivid and unwanted memories that often followed loud noises, the sickening sensation that sent her into spiraling panic, didn't come.

She relaxed a little as she watched more riders pass and then Cameron was there, riding on the wing of a group of cowboys. So that was why he left so early. Why hadn't he said so? He grinned and waved to the crowd, his glance sliding easily over the people lining the route. And her.

It was if he did not recognize her at all. A sudden chill ran down her back, making her shiver in spite of the heat. Puzzled, she watched the group ride away from her. She'd been almost under his nose, for heaven's sake. How could he not have seen her? Or did he not want to?

She stepped back, not caring now who or what came up the street. Had last night been a dream and had what she'd shared with him meant more to her than to him? Could he have forgotten her so easily? And what did it matter anyway? She would soon be gone.

"Idiot," she muttered. "Idiot, idiot, idiot."

She had to get away and pushed through the crowds until she could retreat around the corner. Samantha followed her and caught her arm.

"Trisha, what's up?"

"Didn't you see?" Trisha demanded.

"See what?"

"Cameron. He rode right by and never acknowledged me by so much as blink. You warned me about sexy cowboys but did I listen? Oh, no, not me. Now I feel so, so stupid."

"Maybe he really didn't see you, Trish. Have you any idea how many people are out there?"

Trisha ignored her. "I should never have let that attraction get the better of me. But just for once, I wanted feel pleasure again and not just pain."

"Okay, that comment needs an explanation." Trisha gasped as Samantha grabbed her shoulders and shook her. "You and I hit it off as soon as we met so I consider us friends but now you're holding something back and I need to know what it is." Another shake, gentler this time and Trisha couldn't ignore the genuine concern in Samantha's face. "Trish, I want to help you so just talk to me. Cry on my shoulder if you want to, that's what friends are for."

Trisha swallowed the apprehension that threatened to choke her. Her counselor encouraged her to talk about the incident but each time she tried, her tongue dried and clung to the roof of her mouth just as it did now. She closed her eyes but rather than block out her memories, it only afforded a replay of the worst day of her life.

"Was it really that bad?" Samantha asked, the compassion in her husky voice almost drowned out by a blaring marching band in the background.

"You have no idea," Trisha whispered. "I couldn't believe how blasé I'd been about my life until that crash. It was the end of so much. I can't talk about it, I just can't."

"Whatever, sweetie. But don't forget the saying a trouble shared is a trouble halved, or something like that."

Trisha half smiled at Samantha's insistence. She'd admitted more than she wanted to, but somehow even that made her feel slightly easier. Maybe her counselor was right that letting go, little by little, might just get her past the nightmare her life had become. Behind her a Scottish band marched past and over the skirl of the pipes and rattle and tap of the drums, Samantha grinned at her.

"Hang the parade," she shouted. "Let's go grab lunch or we won't have time to eat until after the publisher's event tonight."

Trisha groaned. "Don't remind me. I've still not forgiven you and I've got butterflies already. What am I supposed to talk about anyway?"

"Your choice, but I'd go heavier on the fashion and celebrity side than anything else. By the way, what do you read?"

"Is that the test question?" Trisha asked as they walked away from the noise and the crowds.

Samantha shook her head. "But it would help if you read some romance."

Trisha made a face. "I have to admit to rarely, if ever. You asked me to look at photos for you. Pick the man who best portrays a romantic image you said, which is subjective to say the least. My idea of a romantic image is likely to be totally different to anyone else's.

That being a given, I can't say any more until I see the photographs. How many are there anyway?"

"Twelve." Samantha said promptly. "After they're unveiled tonight they'll be on display in the Western Art Showcase for the remainder of Stampede. The winner will be announced next Saturday. We're running a draw too, the prize being the book the winner will be featured on, plus dinner with him."

"Hmm." Trisha frowned. "That doesn't sound like much of prize."

"Ah, but the dinner is all expenses paid. So if you win and you're from oh, let's say Australia, that's not a shabby deal at all."

As they walked back to the condo, Trisha agreed that was not in the least shabby. She yawned. Lack of sleep from the previous night was catching up with her. She needed a nap, a shower and then time to conjure up a few words to present to the representatives of the popular publishing house sponsoring the event. Samantha made it all sound simple, even the fact there would be upwards of two hundred people in the audience was a breeze according to her.

No problem. No problem at all.

Trisha fell across her bed and thankfully closed her eyes.

* * *

Cameron stood outside the doors of the hotel's ballroom, waiting impatiently for them to open. People cruised through the main lobby or gathered in groups bathed in subtle lighting from the spectacular chandeliers. Chatter and laughter buzzed around him. He would much rather be out at the ranch, but Greg had given him a ticket for this evening's event and all but begged him to be there.

"Hey, man, I need some support," he'd pleaded and Cameron gave in.

Besides, it would be an opportunity to watch Trisha unobserved. He could stand at the back of the room and maybe learn a little more about her. He'd tried calling her earlier in the day but her phone had been turned off. He hadn't left a message but hoped he'd be able to catch her before the evening ended.

She'd said she was giving a short presentation before introducing the competitors. What was she likely to talk about? He turned to take a short stroll around the lobby rather than continue waiting for the doors to open. The information on his ticket read, 'doors open at six-thirty p.m.' He checked his watch. Ten more minutes. How come he'd arrived so early? Even stopping to shower and shave after the afternoon's steer wrestling event, which he'd won, had taken no time at all.

Intending to kill some time he made for the bar but stopped when he noticed a commotion in the doorway. He groaned inwardly when he recognized the red-head pushing her way aggressively through the crowd and followed her as she marched up to one of the ballroom doors.

"Where are you charging off to in such an all-fired hurry?" He caught her arm and spun her around to face him.

"Get your hands off me, you ...you ..." She kicked at his shins and tried to pull out of his grip.

"Nice to see you too, Donna T." Cameron continued to hold the woman. "Come over here and stop making a spectacle of yourself."

"Spectacle of myself?" Cameron found himself caught in a blaze of bright blue eyes sparking with anger. "Never mind about me, what about my husband? What kind of spectacle is he going to make of himself? Why'd you let him do it, Cameron? Why?"

Cameron edged himself and the petite redhead to the side of the crowd. "I didn't know anything about it until after he'd signed with the modeling agency which helped organize this gig. If he wins it, the prize money will get you out of your hitch with the bank. And if he doesn't, he could still earn a fair few bucks from just modeling. That's why he did it, Donna. For you. So you don't lose your home and livelihood. Can you blame him for that?"

Donna slumped onto a sofa and put her hands over her face. Her bright curls bobbed as she shook her head. "Why didn't he tell me?"

"For exactly this reason." Cameron released her arm once he was sure she wouldn't take another swing at him. "He knew you'd be mad as hell at him and likely try to stop him. All he can see is a big dollar sign if he wins. The book cover is secondary."

"What book cover?" Donna's head snapped up, her eyes narrowed with suspicion.

"All I know is that the competition is sponsored by some publishing house. The winner gets $25,000 and appears on the cover of a western romance novel."

"Western romance?" Donna sprang to her feet. "Is he mad? He knows nothing about romance. Hell, I can't even remember the last time he bought me flowers."

"I don't think he needs to know anything about romance, he just has to look good." Cameron grinned suddenly. "Can't say he's my type, but I guess he might have what it takes. Don't you think he's good looking?"

Donna punched Cameron's upper arm with enough force to make him wince. He rubbed the spot thinking that ranch women never knew their own strength. "Of course I do. That's part of why I married him but I don't want other women looking at him."

"Not even for the prize money?"

"Well," Donna paused, a frown scrunching up her freckled face. "Yeah, I guess that might make a difference."

"Look, there's a dozen photographs in the running. He's got a one-in-twelve chance of walking away with it but no guarantees. Come on, the doors are opening now."

"I want to be right up front and in his face," Donna hissed.

"Not a good idea." Cameron took her arm again as they passed unhindered into the darkened ballroom. "He's going to be as twitchy as treed 'coon. You don't want to rattle him even more and spoil his chances of getting through this evening without egg on his face. Come and sit at the back with me."

Donna relented with a heavy sigh signifying her displeasure and Cameron took her to a table in the far corner of the room. If someone showed up wanting tickets for them both he'd cross that bridge if he came to it. For now he poured them glasses of water from the pitcher on the table while Donna looked nervously towards the stage. Twelve easels set in a semi-circle were already in place. Purple cloths, emblazoned in gold with a double PP interlinked to resemble a cattle brand covered each easel.

Seats were filling fast. People pulled out chairs and seated themselves at the round tables. Donna reached for one of the brochures fanned out at each place setting.

"Oh no." She turned the brochure so that Cameron could see it. "He's not got to compete with this, has he?"

The title on the brochure proclaimed Purple Plain Publishing's selection of its best book covers. Cameron took the brochure, chuckling. The covers showed men with bare chests, impressive abs and bulging biceps.

He laughed aloud and handed the brochure back to Donna. "If you noticed, all these guys have their faces mostly hidden by the brim of their hats. Maybe they're just embarrassed at how they look or maybe those poses are meant to make women drool at their muscles."

Donna flipped his arm with the brochure. "I don't want any other woman drooling over my husband."

"You worried that fame would go to Greg's head?"

Before Donna could answer, the lights in the ballroom dimmed. Cameron looked towards the stage to see what was happening and if he could spot Trisha. A group of smartly dressed people, the men wearing tuxes and the women in evening gowns, filed into the room and took their seats at tables placed front and centre to the stage. They had to be from the publishing company he decided.

A sound technician crossed the stage and checked the microphones. The spotlights flashed on and off, illuminating different areas of the stage and then the backdrop. The technician raised his thumb to someone in the wings.

The lights dimmed even more. Denis Thompson, a local TV personality, bounced on to the stage and took his place in front of the microphone.

"Show time," Cameron muttered.

Chapter Ten

Trisha stood in the wings with butterflies fluttering in the pit of her stomach. She watched Denis playing to the audience. His banter made her smile and the crowd beyond the footlights laughed at his jokes.

Her head still whirled. In the few days since she'd arrived in Calgary she'd been 'duded up' by Samantha, been on a trail ride, seen a cougar, stayed overnight in a remote ranch house and fallen in a love with a cowboy.

Scratch that last thought.

Had sex with a cowboy, she reminded herself. Mind blowing, deeply satisfying sex but that was not love as Samantha had so bluntly reminded her.

So what was it? Trisha could swear that their night together meant as much to Cameron as it had done to her. But then he'd ignored her. Ridden by with a smile on his face and left her with her arm drooping like a flag at half mast. How dumb of her to think it could have been anything else but sex. And he'd got it easy.

She'd dared to step back into life and been given a sharp reminder that along with joy and happiness comes pain, disillusionment and loss. Her loss. Again.

Disappointment manifested itself in a vicious cramp that twisted her gut. She slipped her arm across her stomach and gasped.

"Are you okay, Ms. Watts?" Vince Allen, the stage manager, touched her elbow.

Trisha nodded and whispered back, "Just a bit of stage fright."

Vince grinned at her. "You'll be fine once you get out there. Just look out over the lights. You won't see anyone. It will be like you're on your own. Trust me."

She didn't believe him but thanked him for his reassurance anyway.

"And now, ladies and gentlemen, it's my pleasure to introduce to you the lady who will be the final judge of Purple Plain Publishing's cover models competition."

Trisha looked up in alarm. Final judge? Had she heard correctly? When had that happened? She'd been introduced to Marguerite DeVries, the publisher, only moments before readying herself to come on stage. Marguerite had smiled, shook her hand warmly and thanked her profusely. Now she knew why.

"I'm going to kill her," Trisha muttered viciously, imagining Samantha's demise by several gory and satisfying methods. "Just kill her."

"From London, England, award-winning international photo-journalist, Ms. Trisha Watts." Denis barely took a breath before continuing with her introduction. "Her credits include in-depth looks at subjects as diverse as the Toronto Fashion Week and trail riding in Africa. Along the way she's garnered acclaim for coverage of every aspect of equine sports and more recently some quality time with a Hollywood star that even makes my heart beat faster. And now, ladies and gentlemen, here she is. Ms. Trisha Watts."

Vince gently nudged her arm. "You're on. Go wow them."

Trisha took a deep breath, dreading setting a foot on that stage. Samantha had so much to answer for.

Vince nudged her again and she nodded. She lifted her head, pasted a smile on her face and walked out into the spotlight, waving at the audience as she accepted their applause.

Denis reached in and kissed her on the cheek before leaving her alone in front of the microphone. She adjusted it to her height and as she did so admitted that Vince was right. She looked out into the body of the hall and saw nothing but the dim outline of indeterminate shapes. Only a little light filtered in from the main lobby from around the edges of the draped doors. She hated every minute of it but smiled and thanked Denis and everyone else for the warm welcome.

Once she began to speak, her nervousness dissipated.

"First, I want to assure you that this evening isn't about me or what I have or haven't done." She waited for the burst of appreciative applause to die down. "This is about twelve, handsome, fit young men waiting off-stage ..." catcalls from ladies in the audience had her laughing with genuine amusement.

"I get that you're eager to see them and I can promise you won't be disappointed. These twelve gentlemen have a chance for a prize which could change their lives. If girls and women can make a career out of their looks and style, why shouldn't men?"

She stopped for another round of applause accompanied by rowdy cheers then turned to the first of the easels. As yet she had not seen any of the photographs, and had only rehearsed a few comments with Vince and Samantha for the unveiling of each portrait. She was to locate the name of the subject on the back of the easel and call him on to the stage.

Trisha walked up to the first easel, disliking the purple velvet cover with its cattle-brand logo and tasseled fringe, knowing it was all part and parcel of the build up to revealing the contestants. Never coy or cutesy she now had to be both for Samantha and Marguerite's sake. This was their event, not hers, however underhanded Samantha had been in drawing her into it. Her stomach clenched but she looked over her shoulder at the audience with what she hoped was a saucy grin.

"Are we ready?" she asked and again the reaction from the crowded room rolled over her. She pulled the cover off the first easel, walked behind it and read out the name. "Number One is Brent Heywood. Please come and join me Mr. Heywood."

A tall, slim, dark haired man stepped out onto the stage waving at the crowd with both hands. He topped off the tux he wore with a happy grin on his face. As he stood beside his picture Trisha didn't see a sign of happiness in his ice blue eyes as he continued to wave. She repeated the process with the next three easels, but when she pulled the cover off number five she stopped, sure there had to be a mistake. The first four models were all clothed to some degree, but this guy was buck naked.

His photograph showed him in the shower, one hand splayed across the wall for support while the other held a sponge against his belly. The only screen between the viewer and everything nature blessed him with were the soap suds foaming down his thigh. The stream of water plastered his hair to his head and cascaded off his shoulders. Glistening droplets hung on his eyelashes, barely screening the daring, devil-take-you glint of self mockery she glimpsed in his eyes as he looked straight into the camera.

Shocked, Trisha stepped back and then moved aside so the audience could see the photograph too.

"Number Five," she announced above the hoots and whistles of approval from the ladies. "Mr. Jason Creevey."

* * *

Cameron watched her pull the covers off the easels and drop them with a flick of her fingers as if she didn't like the feel of them. He couldn't blame her. He thought the whole thing tacky but found it hard to take his eyes off her. He hadn't missed the murmurs of appreciation when she'd walked on stage either. When he looked around at the men close to him he saw that they all stared at Trisha. Her simple black lace dress clung to her lithe body leaving little to the imagination. Her legs looked longer and slimmer because of the black high heels she wore. She'd changed her hair style again with bangs now shielding her forehead and the rest of her hair pulled back into a high, sleek pony tail showing off her long, slim neck.

"I hate her," Donna T muttered.

"Why?" Cameron couldn't take his eyes off the figure on the stage.

"Well, look at her. She's tall and slim and gorgeous and sometime very soon my husband is probably going to be up close and personal with her."

"Calm down, Donna." Cameron gave her hand a friendly squeeze. "I know for a fact Greg's not her type. She's just doing a job."

Donna squinted at him. "How would you know that?"

"Hush up now." Cameron had no intention of giving anything away to Donna and simply nodded towards the stage.

They'd watched the first four competitors without comment, but when Trisha announced Number Five, Donna groaned.

"Trust Jason Creevey to get in there," she muttered. "If he's in the running there's not a chance for anyone else. Poor Greg."

Trisha continued to remove the covers and call out names until there was only one competitor left. With a flourish she whipped away the cover on the last easel and made a great show of looking at the name on the back of it.

"Ladies and Gentleman," she spoke clearly into her hand held mic, "May I present to you competitor Number Twelve, Mr. Greg Tooley."

Greg walked out onto the stage and Donna's hands flew to cover her face. Finally she dared to look and when she did Cameron heard her gasp.

"He's wearing a tux." She turned to him in astonishment. "He doesn't even own a tux. Where would he have got that?"

"They were probably all sent to the same tux rental outfit by the publishing house's PR people," Cameron told her. "Have to say he cleans up purdy good, doncha think?"

By way of an answer to his exaggerated drawl Donna thumped him again. Cameron sighed and rubbed his arm.

"You really have got to stop doing that Donna, or I'll be black and blue come morning. Come on, I want to introduce you to someone."

Cameron gave her no time to argue. He hauled her to her feet and headed towards the front of the ballroom. Trisha stood to one side of the stage talking to a group of people. They faded into obscurity as he focused on her, seeing only the pale oval of her face and the dark smudges under her eyes.

Anger tightened his jaw. Couldn't these people see how tired she was? Reason told him he was over reacting, but what had reason to do with the fierce stab of jealousy that walloped his solar plexus as suddenly and hard as a well placed hoof? As he came closer, Trisha looked up.

A flash of anger flared in her eyes when she spotted him but then she blinked and forced a tight, uncertain smile. Other than having to leave in such a hurry this morning, he couldn't think of anything he'd done to make her so obviously angry.

Two of the competitors who'd been in the group talking to her, both of whom Cameron knew slightly, moved away as he and Donna pressed forward. The last time Cameron had seen Trisha she'd been dressed in a towel. Now her fancy duds somehow affected the way his tongue worked.

"Donna barrel races," he told Trisha after he'd finally got his mouth to cooperate again and finished introducing them to each other. "You might want to set up an interview with her for your article."

"Why don't you come to our barbeque tomorrow night and interview me then?" Donna, having swallowed her initial resentment looked hopeful, then disappointed when Trisha shook her head.

"I would enjoy that, but it could be a little awkward. I'm still not sure of my actual role for this event but interviewing a competitor's wife might be construed as conflict of interest."

Trisha flashed an apologetic smile at Donna, ignored Cameron, and moved away to join one of the publishing house reps.

Cameron frowned as he watched her weave her way easily between a few people to meet the man who had caught her attention. That stab of jealousy wormed its way under his ribs again, making him catch his breath. He let it go in a grunt when Donna planted her elbow into his side.

"Roll up your tongue, cowboy," she said with a chuckle. "She's out of your league."

"Ya think?"

"I know," Donna declared. "Louboutin's and ranching aren't exactly a match made in heaven."

"What the heck are Louboutin's?" Cameron asked.

"Shoes, dummy." Donna rolled her eyes at his ignorance. "Classy, designer shoes. Think the cost of a good quarter horse stud fee, if not more."

Cameron's jaw dropped. "You're kidding, right?"

"Nope. Hey, there's Greg."

Cameron recovered his jaw while Donna, in spite of her earlier fury, greeted her husband with a whoop and a big hug. Cameron heard her mutter something about Greg being a crazy galoot but loving him all the more for it.

"Thanks for being here, buddy." Greg reached out a hand to Cameron.

"Wouldn't have missed it for the world." Cameron took his hand but pulled Greg in to a back slapping hug. "Donna provided one half of the show, you the other. What happens now?"

"I'm going to take him home and peel that tux off of him."

Donna's saucy little giggle and Greg's answering grin left Cameron in doubt of their intentions.

"Okay, guys, that's a bit too much information for me. I'm gone."

* * *

With a pang of envy Trisha watched Cameron tip his hat to the red-headed girl. He appeared to be comfortable around everyone she'd seen him with so far. Being warm to her one minute and cutting her off cold the next totally confused her. Nor had she seen him treat anyone else in such a cavalier fashion.

If she had any sense she'd ignore him in the same way he'd ignored her. Too bad that part of her well, she might as well admit it, all of her, craved his presence. Talk about asking to be let down. Disgusted with herself she turned and almost immediately bumped into Brent Heywood. She stepped back with a sudden gasp, unable to stifle the dismay she felt at his closeness. The moment he'd stepped on the stage when she'd uncovered his picture her skin had tingled with an unpleasant premonition.

"Enjoying the view of Number Twelve?" He appeared to not notice her reaction at being so close to him and nodded his head towards Greg.

"He's certainly a good looking man," Trisha agreed, "but spoken for. The girl with him is his wife."

"And the other guy?" Brent asked.

"A friend of Greg and Donna's I believe."

"Hm. Getting mighty friendly with the locals, aren't we?" Brent's tone held a barely disguised sneer.

"It's my job to be friendly." Trisha made her voice non-committal as Brent walked around her as stealthily as a prowling cat.

She turned to face him, instantly aware that in doing so her back was to the room. Intuition told her that he wanted her full attention. Not wishing to give him that satisfaction, she stepped to his left and turned so that she could see several of the tables and the guests sitting at them.

Smiling, Brent leant towards her. "Then be friendly," he whispered. "Patricia."

Hearing her given name delivered in such a chilling manner shocked Trisha into immobility.

"Nothing to say?" Brent persisted when she didn't respond. "Please tell me I haven't got it wrong. It is Patricia Somerville, isn't it? Contender for the European three-day event championships. Until you killed your horse that is. What was his name? Oh, yes. Delacourt."

Trisha didn't even have to close her eyes to see again her beautiful thoroughbred gelding prancing across the green turf, his neck arched and his black hide gleaming as it slid easily over his well toned muscles. Honest and brave, the best horse she'd ever had.

Brent made an expressive gesture with his hand. Any onlooker might assume he was explaining something to her with great good humor. Only she could see the steely glint in his pale blue eyes, a glacial contrast to the happy smile plastered on his face.

"Still nothing to say?" He bumped his shoulder gently against hers but there was nothing gentle in his cold tone. "People here in Stampede City are very serious about horses. They wouldn't take to someone who'd caused their horse's death. So consider being very friendly to me Ms. Somerville. One word in the right ears would open a can of worms I think you'd rather not deal with."

Trisha licked her lips nervously. "How do you expect me to do anything for you when I'm not judging this competition?" She hated hearing the quaver in her own voice.

"Oh, but I have it on the best authority that you are. I spoke to Marguerite DeVries just before I came on stage and she's just thrilled you agreed to be the judge."

Trisha's head reeled with anger at Samantha. How could looking at photographs of cowboys for the modeling agency have escalated so quickly to picking the winner for a publishing house's cover competition, the latter without her knowledge or her consent? Her mind conjured up all manner of retribution to be heaped on Samantha at the earliest opportunity. But right now she had to deal with Brent Heywood.

"What do you want?" she asked, although she was sure of the answer.

"First place of course." Brent shifted as if to move away from her but then zeroed in again and shook her hand. Her skin crawled at his touch. "Just remember Delacourt."

Nausea threatened to swamp her and she gripped the back of the closest chair. She tried to not gasp for breath and hoped that no one would see her distress as she sank onto the seat. She poured herself a glass of water from the jug on the table and took one sip, then another. Before she knew it she had drained the glass.

"Nerves got the better of you, Ms. Watts?" Vince Allen drew up a chair beside her. "Or are those shoes getting uncomfortable?"

"Both," Trisha admitted, thankful for the distraction his attention offered her. "And I must say thank you for your advice to me at the beginning of this evening. It helped a lot."

"Here's a bit more, if you'd like it." Vince watched her with steady eyes.

"What would that be?" She caught her breath. As if dealing with Brent Heywood wasn't bad enough, did she have to repel attackers from other sides too?

"I saw Heywood talking to you," Vince said. "I got the impression from the look on your face you weren't happy with what he had to say. There's no good news around that man. You'd best stay away from him altogether if you can."

Trisha bit her lip and nodded. "Were there any cameras on us Vince? Could anyone else have seen what you did?"

Vince shook his head. "The news crews have all gone and everyone else has wrapped. Can't guarantee no one might have got you on a cell phone, but if they did and there's any questions you can always say you were tired."

"And that would be true." Trisha stood and straightened her dress. "On that note, I think I'm going to call it a night."

"Want me to get you a cab?"

Trisha's phone vibrated inside her clutch purse. She withdrew it, saw who the text was from and shook her head.

"Thanks, Vince, but no. It's taken care of."

"Then I'll say goodnight." Vince smiled at her and stood up. "See you next week for the presentations."

Trisha waited until he was out of earshot and then pressed her speed dial. "Are you still here?"

Cameron heard the edge of panic in her voice. "Yep. Just at the main door. Do you want me to wait for you?"

"Please." She disconnected.

Cameron slipped the phone back in his pocket. She'd obviously been on edge when they'd been talking with Donna and Greg. Then she'd left them to join the publishing rep. What could have changed in so short a time? He turned back from the entrance doors. Being tall had its advantages and he soon spotted her as she hurried out of the ballroom.

She looked right and left, obviously looking for him. He moved towards her, shocked to see her tightly drawn expression. He stepped in front of her and caught her by the shoulders.

"Hey, going my way?" he asked gently.

"On this occasion, yes." She dropped her forehead against his chest and briefly leaned into him. "Thank you for waiting for me. Could we get a drink?"

"Sure." Curious about what other occasion she referred to, right now Cameron only cared that she was with him. "Would you like to go to the lounge here or do you want to go somewhere else?"

"Here will be fine."

Taking her elbow he steered her into the hotel's elegant lounge bar. A couple left a corner table and he quickly snagged it. Trisha sank into the chair he held for her. He didn't like the wan expression on her face but before he could ask her any questions the waitress arrived to take their order.

"White wine, please." Trisha crossed her arms across her chest.

Cameron ordered a beer for himself and watched her as she fought to regain some composure. He sat back, not wanting to crowd her. She'd been fine this morning then seemed upset with him this evening and he still couldn't figure out why.

"Want to tell me what upset you?"

She rested her elbow on the table, then placed her chin on her upturned hand and looked at him with troubled eyes. "I can't."

"Can't or won't?" Cameron countered. He watched her close her eyes and slowly shake her head. She licked her lips and his heart almost went into overdrive as he remembered what that sexy little tongue could do.

"If I tell you, I think you'll just get mad," she said.

"Try me."

Trisha hesitated. She couldn't deny that he made her blood sing and her pulse race, and that she somehow breathed more easily when in his company. But how could she make him understand something she didn't fully understand herself? Liking him, lusting over him, wanting to be with him didn't mean she could or should trust him. She'd trusted once before and still carried that hurt with her. Maybe

Samantha had been right, there were just too many people in that crowd this morning for him to have seen her. But why didn't he tell her before he left that he was riding in the parade? She pushed her thoughts aside, knowing that Cameron waited for her answer.

"If you must know," she said hesitantly, "I'm glad you were still here because I feel safe with you. That is so illogical because we've only just met, but it's true."

"I'll take that as a compliment and thank you for it." Cameron watched her play with the stem of her wine glass. "Why didn't you feel safe?"

Trisha lifted her eyes to his as if to gauge his reaction.

"I let one of the contestants rattle me. It's really nothing but I didn't want to walk out of here on my own."

A slow burn of anger ignited in the pit of Cameron's stomach and his hand tightened on the beer bottle he held. Jealousy had never been one of his issues, but now every time he thought of Trisha with someone else it made him grit his teeth. He simply did not understand how one night with her had so completely turned his world upside down.

When he looked at her his brain became jumbled with a series of fanciful images. He saw her with him beside a cozy fire, working side by side getting a meal ready, laughing together in the barn. Hell, he saw himself married to her for goodness sake, an institution he'd never even considered when friends like Greg and Donna Tooley tied the knot. Marriage had been something that might happen one day when he had the security of a home and a business behind him. He carefully put his bottle down on the table.

"Which one of them was it?"

Trisha leaned in towards him. "Promise me you won't do anything stupid. Please."

Cameron gave her his assurance that he wouldn't leap to his feet, charge out of the lounge and tear the man's head from his shoulders.

"The very first guy out of the box. Brent Heywood." Trisha sipped her wine and licked her lips again.

Cameron wished she would stop doing that. "What did he do?"

"It wasn't so much what he did as what he said." She shrugged and rubbed a hand across her forehead. "I'm sorry. I'm really making a fuss about nothing. I must be tired."

Cameron took a pull on his beer, mulling over what she'd said. He knew she must have some baggage to act the way she sometimes did. Could Heywood possibly know something about her background and have challenged her with it? He had so many questions but now was not the time to ask them. She said she felt safe with him and that, for now, was enough. He let the beer trickle slowly down his throat while he reined in his thoughts.

"You haven't really had time to slow down, have you?" he asked casually.

"Not much." Trisha actually managed a regretful chuckle. "Would you please just take me home? I think Brent's already left but I don't want any trouble. Marguerite DeVries doesn't deserve to have her hard work jeopardized by someone with an over inflated ego."

"You think I have an over inflated ego?" Cameron pretended to be wounded by her comment.

"No, silly." Trisha said with a chuckle at his teasing. "But Brent Heywood does. Yes, he's good looking and very photogenic. Because of that he thinks he can charm me into bending the rules. I really didn't like refusing your friend's invitation to that barbeque but until I can talk to Samantha and Marguerite together, I'm not even entirely sure I know where I fit in to their scheme."

"I know Samantha's your friend but she seems to be more than a little devious, and don't worry about Donna. She's cool." Cameron made no comment of the fact that Trisha had totally ignored him during that little exchange and he still couldn't figure out why. He picked up the filmy wrap she'd thrown over the arm of the chair and draped it around her shoulders.

As they left the lounge he took her arm. If Brent Heywood lurked anywhere in the lobby he hoped it would give him fair warning that Trisha was not alone.

Once they reached his truck, Cameron looked down at the short, tight skirt of her dress that skimmed her flat stomach and flowed over her hips as smoothly as liquor over ice.

"I was going to say hop in," he joked as he unlocked the truck, "but I guess I'd better lift you."

He felt her hesitation but then she wound her arms around his neck and relaxed into him as he picked her up. He cradled her for a moment, inhaling the alluring floral scent of her hair and skin.

"Whose home do you want to go to?" he whispered against her temple.

Trisha closed her eyes. Still disconcerted by Brent Heywood, still furious with Samantha for elbowing her into a role she did not want nor had agreed to, Cameron's gentleness acted on her like balm. After the way she had almost snarled at him earlier she hadn't expected him to be so kind. He had shown her by look and touch that he cared about her. That would be something to cherish. They only had a few more days together. Why not make perfect memories while she could? She simply could give him only one answer.

"Yours, please."

He placed her onto the passenger seat and kissed her, letting his lips slide gently across hers then linger as he teased her mouth with the tip of his tongue. He sensed her smile, heard her satisfied intake of breath as she responded, then he pulled away and looked into her eyes.

"You are quite the lady. You know that, right?" he said softly.

"I'm glad you think so." Her reply was just as soft.

He closed the door, and went around to the driver's side, his heart hammering and his palms moist. In a slight daze, he realized that no woman had ever really mattered to him before he'd met Ms. Watts. Right now he was treading dangerous waters and completely out of his depth.

"I have to be at the Stampede for about noon tomorrow," he told her. "I'll drop you back at the condo on my way so you can change. I can't see you tramping around in those spikes."

Trisha laughed as she relaxed back in her seat. "They are actually more comfortable than they look. But you're right, I will need to change into something more suitable for daytime wear."

They completed the drive in silence, which soon evaporated when they pulled up in front of the house and the dogs came tearing to greet them. When Cameron finished petting them, he opened the passenger door for her. Despite the doubts that still crept into her mind from time to time, she slipped happily into his arms. He held her close, nuzzling her shoulder before releasing her but she'd twined her arms around his neck and hung on as she slid slowly down his body, each undulation a sinewy reminder of what she was capable of doing to him. She laughed with delight at her effectiveness when he groaned out loud.

"I was going to ask if you wanted a drink but now you don't get a choice. I am taking you straight to bed." His warm breath tickled her ear.

She pulled off her shoes and swung them by the heels as she followed him along the veranda and into his bedroom. He didn't switch on any lights as he took her straight to his bed where he drew back the comforter. When he turned around she already had her back to him ready for him to unzip her dress.

"It scares me that this feels so right," she whispered more to herself than him as he kissed the back of her neck.

He ran the zipper down and slipped the dress from her shoulders then helped her shrug the fabric away from her arms. Dropping a kiss on her shoulder, he closed his eyes as he ran his hands around her sides, skimming over her silky skin and up over her ribs until he cupped her bare breasts. She quivered at his touch and when his teeth gently grazed her neck, her soft moan became a cry of pleasure. Reluctant to release her, he used one hand to push the dress down over her hips. As the fabric crumpled in soft folds around her feet she stepped out of it and turned to him, nestling her head into his chest and holding him tight.

"Get into bed," he said in a voice thick with longing.

She shimmied under the comforter. How many more nights might they have together like this? Trisha sighed. She would make their loving sweet and fun. Seconds later she threw her black lace thong at him.

"Ms. Watts, you are one hell of a tease." He chuckled and slipped into bed beside her.

He drew her into his arms, felt the coolness of her body against the heat of his as she climbed on top of him. She traced his lips with her forefinger and he gently caught it between his teeth, then drew it into his mouth and sucked hard. He felt her sigh through the whole length of her body then she withdrew her finger and placed her mouth gently on his.

What started as a tender kiss quickly escalated into the exquisite passion they shared the previous night. Hands held, explored, touched and teased. Mouths met and tongues tangled, bodies strained for the release that each could give the other. In the quiet aftermath, while their breath slowed and their pulses returned to normal, they simply held each other.

Trisha didn't want to talk. That she had given in so quickly to her heart and body's demands unnerved her and she still had to come to terms with the emotions Cameron prompted in her. But not now, not right this minute. She gave a contented sigh and turned on her side.

Cameron threw an arm over her and pulled her against his body, spooning her gently until they both slipped in to a deep sleep.

Chapter Eleven

The sky could not have been bluer or provided such a perfect backdrop for the magnificent country mansion in her peripheral vision. She refocused on the jump ahead of her, a log into a green lane, a post and rail fence out of it on the far side. Room for two strides between them but Delacourt stumbled before the log. She held him up, steadied him and he soared over the obstacle and then was falling ...

"No, no. I was wrong. I'm sorry, so sorry."

Trisha's head rolled against the pillow and the sob that caught in her throat woke Cameron. He bolted upright in bed, and turned on the night lamp. In the soft light that fell across her face he saw the sheen of perspiration on her forehead and the flush in her cheeks. He caught her arms but she twisted away from him.

"Leave me alone. Get off me, get off me!" Her voice rose and Cameron caught her again, this time folding his arms around her and holding her tightly. She sobbed against his chest and he continued to hold her until the sobs subsided and she settled back into a semblance of sleep.

Shaken by the extreme fear he sensed in her, he lay back against the pillows. He still held her close, listening to the mutterings under her breath, feeling the echoes of panic in the grip of her fingers and nervous shift of her legs.

He glanced at the clock on the nightstand which showed five-thirty a.m. He had to take her back to the condo before going to the Stampede so saw no point in trying to go back to sleep now. He lay quietly, thinking back to the night she had slept alone in his bed.

Her sleep had been disturbed that night. He remembered how her fingers twitched and her head had tossed restlessly on the pillow, the vague mutterings that he could make no sense of. Did it have anything to do with what she'd hinted at last night?

He closed his eyes and listened to her breathing steady until it became deep and even. He felt her relax as he held her close. At least he could offer her that, because he would indeed do everything possible to keep her safe. That vulnerability he'd sensed in her when he'd first met her tugged at his heart. That she trusted him was a bonus.

He looked at the clock again, decided he should get up and gently disentangled himself from Trisha's warmth. Grabbing his jeans, he pulled them on as he went through to the kitchen where he quickly filled the coffee maker. He left it to brew and went outside to feed the dogs.

There was logic in his normal daily routine that helped ground him, for he could make no sense at all of his whirling emotions about Trisha. He ran his hand through his hair until it stood up in short, messy spikes and huffed a breath of frustration between his lips. He hadn't been so knocked sideways since Mackenzie upped and left him to deal with the mess caused by their parents' death.

"We don't need any distractions, do we boys?" he murmured to the dogs as he petted them, all the while thinking of the distraction still in his bed.

He straightened up as he heard the door open behind him. Trisha, wrapped in his black robe, stepped out hesitantly onto the veranda.

"Mind if I join you?"

That she had to ask made him think she'd overheard his comment to the dogs.

"Take a seat and I'll get the coffee. Cream, no sugar. Right?"

Trisha nodded and he frowned when he saw the blue shadows under her eyes. When he came back from the kitchen she'd settled herself in a cedar Adirondack chair.

"I hope I didn't disturb you last night." She took her coffee from him but avoided his eyes. "I don't think I slept very well."

"You were a bit restless." He smiled at her. "Nothing I couldn't handle."

"But you need your sleep if you're to compete efficiently. I shouldn't have come out here last night."

He looked at her over the rim of his mug but she'd bowed her head and he could see nothing of her face, only the fall of her bangs across her forehead. "Are you saying that was a bad thing?"

"No, not exactly." Hesitation lingered in her voice as if she chose her words carefully. "But I haven't taken one photograph or a written a word since I arrived. I got sidetracked with that event last night and should get back to the real reason I'm here and let you get on with your work."

"That sounds like a brush off to me." He carefully placed his mug on the veranda rail although he could just as easily have thrown it against the wall in frustration.

"Cameron," Trisha didn't look at him but watched her fingers as she ran them around the rim of her mug. "You make me feel things I shouldn't feel, make me want things I can't have. I will go back to London and continue with my life when Stampede is over and you have your horses and your ranch to take care of. I think we should just concentrate on what we have to do."

"So you don't want to see me anymore." He sagged back against a veranda post, not believing she could mean what he heard her say. Frustration segued into a cold anger, anger that she would so easily write off what they might have together.

"I'm sorry if I mislead you." Trisha bit her lip and added in what appeared as almost an afterthought, "I think I mislead myself."

Cameron looked at the coffee in his mug as if it had turned to sludge. Whatever thoughts he'd had, whatever hopes he may have harbored in the last few days, evaporated from his mind as quickly as dew on a summer morning. He looked at Trisha's bent head, watched the way she played with her mug and knew with certainty she'd felt the same things he had. He pursed his lips as he looked at her. Hell, no way was he going to let her off lightly.

"You're scared," he accused. She looked up at that. Damn, but her eyes should not be moss-bright in the morning sun, should not be looking at him like he was breakfast. "You're saying one thing but I think you mean another. If you feel whatever we've got is moving too fast, I'd agree with you. We met five days ago and already I can't imagine my life without you. How do you think that makes me feel?"

Trisha shrugged. Cameron took her mug from her hand and set it on the arm of the chair then hauled her to her feet into a warm embrace. Her heart beat rapidly as her arms snaked around his waist and she rested her head on his shoulder.

"Don't pretend you couldn't care less," he growled softly. "For both our sakes be honest. If you really don't want to see me again, then I suppose I'll have to live with that. But if you feel anything close to what I do, then we'll find a way to make it work."

For a moment Trisha didn't dare believe what she heard. He'd voiced the same doubts she had. And not see him again? Of course she wanted to see him again. As for making a relationship work when distance was involved, hadn't her parents shown her that was possible?

"Promise?" she whispered.

"Promise." He kissed the top of her head and he heard her sniff. "But not if you cry."

"I'm not crying," she said with a shaky laugh, "but you're right. I am scared and I don't know what to do."

"So running away from whatever we have before we figure it out makes sense?"

"I guess not."

"Okay." Cameron kissed her again, then chucked her chin to make sure she was looking at him. "Hey, trust me?" She nodded. "Good. Then we can talk later. There isn't time right now, we have to get going. I can shower first, or you can, or we can take a shower together."

Trisha came close to chuckling. "If we have to get going the last option is no option at all. I think I'm more shower ready than you, so I'll go first. Too bad I don't have jeans and a shirt with me, my dress is likely more than a little wrinkled this morning."

"And I don't do ironing but while you shower I'll make toast and eggs."

Cameron hummed an old country and western tune as he worked around the kitchen. By the time the toaster popped, Trisha had finished her shower and slipped back into her dress as easily as she'd slipped out of it the previous night. Cameron zipped it up reluctantly then headed to the bathroom for his shower while Trisha ate her breakfast.

She rinsed the plates and mugs and collected her shoes and wrap. Cameron had already made the bed and in no time they were ready to leave.

As they hit the highway Trisha realized how easy their preparations had been. There had been no hitches, each doing simple things with no discussion and without getting in each other's way. It was almost too easy, too orchestrated as if they had been doing it all their lives. She looked across at Cameron, at his firm jaw, at the sturdy column of his neck and the curl of hair beneath the top button of his shirt. He was so familiar to her, as if he'd stamped his character on her the moment he touched her in the store.

And if he was to be believed, he felt the same about her. She rubbed her forehead to erase the negative thoughts that lingered there. Her past had an uncanny knack of jumping into the present but, if she was to have any chance at a life that could pass as normal, she had to deal with it.

Cameron drew her out of her daydream when he pulled into the curb outside the condo building. Ever the gentlemen he opened the truck door, waited while she pushed her feet into her shoes then walked with her across the sidewalk to the entrance door.

"I have no idea how you can walk in those things," he said with a grin, "but I sure like what they do for your legs."

"That's the general idea of high heels." For the first time that morning Trisha laughed. "Best of luck for your event today. Will I see you later?"

"I'll call you. We should go to the Ranchman's tonight. It'll be noisy, but might give you some background material for your article. Think you'll be up for it?"

Trisha accepted his invitation without hesitation and he gave her a parting kiss on the cheek. All gentle, loving thoughts of Cameron began to fade as she keyed in the door code. By the time she reached the apartment she seethed with resentment at her friend's deceptiveness.

"Morning Sweetie." Samantha, wearing pink pyjamas, her dark hair still tousled from bed, smiled artlessly and greeted her from where she sat curled up on her sofa.

"Don't you Sweetie me," Trisha snapped, fisting her hands on her hips. "After last night I don't even know how to speak to you, you made me so angry. Do you mind telling me exactly what you expect me to do? If you can possibly manage it, the truth would be extremely helpful."

"You'll just get more irate than you already are." Samantha didn't sound at all repentant as she looked Trisha over. "God, don't tell me you slept in my designer dress."

Trisha threw her hands up in exasperation. "To hell with the dress. I'm warning you, Samantha Monroe—"

"Or are you going to tell me you didn't sleep at all?"

"Will you please tell me what's going on?" Trisha huffed. "Or am I really going mad?"

Samantha unwound herself from her seat, stood up and reached for Trisha's hands.

"You're not going mad, Trish, and you probably won't like it but come and sit down and I promise I'll explain everything."

"You are such a bag," Trisha complained but allowed herself to be drawn to the zebra-printed sofa.

"After you phoned about coming to stay with me, I called your parents." Samantha lifted a warning finger when Trisha opened her mouth to speak. "Yell at me if you must when you've heard me out. You sounded so disoriented that I wanted to know how you really were. You never told me exactly what happened after the crash and I didn't want to push. Not then. Your parents were so worried about you and knew you wouldn't listen to them but might listen to me. They think you've sunk too far into yourself. I do too. Pushing you in a round-about way seemed a sensible thing to do. I'd have got you on a horse again with or without Cameron Carter. And getting you in front of that crowd last night was part of trying to get you to see yourself for who you really are. Now, if I'd laid all that out for you up front, what would you have done?"

"You didn't even give me a choice." Trisha crossed her arms over her chest and looked down at her feet.

"But if I had?" Samantha persisted. "What would you have done?"

Trisha continued to hang her head.

"Come on, Trish, time to 'fess up."

"Stop bullying me," Trisha mumbled.

"Then answer me." Samantha gently shook her shoulder.

"Oh, enough already." Trisha sprang to her feet and paced the floor. "I'd have refused. Happy now?"

"Not entirely, but I think we're beginning to get somewhere."

"You sound just like my counselor," Trisha complained.

"And how're those sessions working out for you?" Samantha cocked her head to one side like a curious bird while she waited for a response.

"Not as progressive as I'd hoped." Trisha admitted with a sigh and sat down again. "I just can't get past the nightmares and sharp, loud noises bring everything back as if it's happening all over again and then, if I can't catch my breath or control myself in time, I simply pass out. You have no idea how disconcerting and embarrassing that is."

"No, I don't. I can only imagine." Samantha gave Trisha's hand a comforting squeeze. "Want coffee?"

"No, thank you, and I haven't finished with you yet either."

Samantha raised an eyebrow then fluffed up her bed-head. "Okay, go ahead and slap my wrists but while you're doing it remember that I only had your best interests at heart."

"That maybe so, but now I have a problem that's going to impact you and Marguerite and this damn competition. You should have been straight with me about what you wanted me to do. Finding out in a room full of people that I'm the final judge has put me in a situation I don't want to handle."

"What do you mean?"

"Brent Heywood." Trisha ran the back of her hand across her forehead as if just saying his name gave her a headache. "He knows who I am and what happened. He threatened to make it public if I don't pick him as the winner. My situation could wreck any credibility your competition might have."

Samantha got to her feet, frowning as she recalled the contestants. The moment she remembered Brent Heywood her mouth tightened. "I knew I didn't like him. Nice smile on his face but not in his eyes."

"That's the one. We are going to have to talk to Marguerite."

"I'll call her." Samantha pulled her phone out of her briefcase and hastily pressed buttons. "I have to be down at the grounds this afternoon to meet Purple Plain's cover designer, Patsy Livingstone. The photo display went up in the

Western Art exhibition at some ungodly hour last night and she wants to see them in all their full blown glory."

She stopped and held up a finger to indicate her call had connected. "Hi Marguerite. Are you free this afternoon? No? Okay, then it will have to be tomorrow. Yes, my office. Two o'clock. Bye."

She snapped the phone shut. "Did Brent threaten you physically?"

"No, he didn't have to. Making my past public when I've tried so hard to put it behind me is all the threat he needed, and he knew it." Trisha shivered with foreboding and folded her arms across her chest. "If only I could go back to that day and make a different decision."

"Sweetie, you can't, and torturing yourself about it now won't change that." Samantha spoke softly as she laid her hand on Trisha's arm. "No one blames you but you. Now, if you don't have any plans for today, you should come with me because I don't like leaving you on your own."

Trisha gave a suspicious sniff but her eyes were dry. "I've nothing until this evening. Apparently I'm being taken to the Ranchman's."

"Cameron warned you it will be bursting at the seams, right?"

"No, but I can imagine. By the way, is this Art exhibition a dressy affair?"

"Nope. Just wear western and you'll be good for the rest of the day."

* * *

Samantha groaned as she got out of her car. "Hot, hot, hot. Thank god for my sunglasses and hat. Have you got the bottles of water?"

"No, you have." Trisha watched with amusement as Samantha shuffled through the debris on the back seat, grabbing papers and transferring them to a large shoulder bag where she had stashed the precious water.

Muttering that she really should clean out her car, Samantha finally organized herself and slammed the doors shut.

"Right." She looked around to get her bearings. "The BMO Centre is this way. Got your pass?"

Trisha reached for the ID hanging around her neck and flashed it under Samantha's nose. "If I get lost shall I find a nice policeman?"

"Yes, and make sure you get your ice cream."

Samantha waded into the crowd and Trisha, chuckling, followed her. Sneak-a-Peek, she realized, had simply been an appetizer. This was the main course. Wherever she looked there was something to see. Kiosks full of soft toys and outrageous cowboy hats vied with booths offering a variety of games. People stood in line for food from pizza slices to hamburgers. Chatter and laughter buzzed around her and a huge roar of applause billowed up from beyond the grandstand in response to whatever event took place there.

She hurried after Samantha into the cool interior of the exhibition hall, glad of the respite both from the heat and the noise. Here the colors were muted, the conversation a murmur not a crashing wall of sound as outside. She looked in at the booths they passed, intrigued by the quality of the art work on display. Many of the paintings gave her the impression she could just step into them and the sculptures were so life-like she was almost disappointed to feel cool metal beneath her hand and not flesh-and-blood hair and hide.

"Ah, here we are." Samantha stopped and looked up at the wall behind several booths displaying handicrafts. She quickly scanned the aisles either side of her. "Not the best location, but at least there's room for these blown up posters and they can be clearly seen. Purple Plain should be pleased. Hang on here, I'm going to get us a drink."

Samantha veered off into the crowd without giving Trisha a chance to comment but that gave her time to catch her breath and inspect the photographs once more. She perched on the end of a bench from where she could watch people as they looked up at the posters. Their comments swung from 'yum' to 'practically porn' as many of them filled in entry slips for the prize draw.

"They look good don't they? I think I could use any one of them for a Purple Plain cover."

Trisha turned to find Patsy beside her. "Will you?"

"Of course. That's the beauty of this competition." Patsy subjected each poster to a closer inspection. "If the contestants do enter into a contract with Samantha's agency, they have to also accept the clause giving Purple Plain exclusivity for one year. It means these guys can't market themselves until the contract is fulfilled."

"Is that good?"

"You bet it is," Patsy said. "The trouble with the open photo stock I work from is that everyone can use it. We want our covers to be distinctive, and if the model is on half a dozen different covers in whatever pose, you lose that distinction. I thought about taking photographs for my own use, but I simply don't have the time for it."

"Samantha will have these boys under contract in no time at all," Trisha said with a laugh, "and then you can work with her."

"Are you taking my name in vain?" Samantha arrived with the drinks and sat down beside Trisha.

"I wouldn't dream of it, but I do see Patsy's point. I can't even begin to imagine how many photographs may be out there or how difficult it is for you to pick the right model for the right cover. I'm glad I just take photos."

"Oh, excuse me, I see a client I need to talk to." Samantha was on her feet, wine glass in hand.

"Is that woman ever still?" Patsy asked as Samantha merged into the crowd again.

"I'd guess only when she's asleep." Trisha picked up her wine.

"So talking of taking photos," Patsy persisted, "you could photograph the models Samantha signs up for us. Especially someone like him, with or without his shirt. If you could do that you'd be my best friend forever."

Trisha caught the lascivious gleam in Patsy's eye and looked over her shoulder.

There was no mistaking the height and build of the cowboy strolling along the aisle. Everything about him made Trisha's pulse flutter. Her mouth curved into an involuntary smile as she watched him looking at the art work on offer on either side of him.

She couldn't prevent the warm current of happiness that swept over her as he got closer. He stopped at a booth to look at some leather face masks and anticipation bubbled in her stomach. She got to her feet, ready to excuse herself from Patsy's company but then her jaw sagged in disbelief.

Her heart lurched, skipped a beat then pounded painfully against her ribs at what she saw.

Chapter Twelve

A slim blonde girl, whose bare and tanned mile-long legs emerged from tight denim shorts, caught up with Cameron and grabbed his arm. Trisha heard his unmistakable laughter as he held a mask up for the girl's inspection.

The wine glass almost fell from her hand as she watched in awful disbelief as the girl reached up on tip-toe and kissed him on the cheek. Cameron wrapped his arm around her waist, hugged her to him and kissed her back.

Ocean waves couldn't have risen and fallen as quickly as did the joy in her heart. This could not be happening. She turned to face the posters, blocking out the sound of the girl's giggles as she and Cameron passed behind her.

She tried to shut out the image of the blonde girl's off-the-shoulder white Mexican style blouse, shorts and pink cowboy boots. How tasteless were they, or did Cameron think them cute? If that's what he wanted, then he was welcome to it.

Humiliation warmed her face. Tears stung her eyes. She blinked them back.

How could he pretend they might have something together and accuse her of being scared when he had another woman on his arm?

She blinked furiously and swallowed hard. No way would she shed one single tear for him or what might have been. The burn in her lungs threatened to choke her and the crushing pain in her chest could only be her heart breaking. Every thought, every hope she'd allowed herself to think or feel in the past few days crowded into her head making it spin. She had no one to blame but herself. She'd let herself be drawn in by a sexy smile and a warm touch, by the dream of a future that could never be. She wanted nothing more now than to cut and run, but to where?

She took a deep breath, hoping that Patsy hadn't noticed her distress.

"So what would you think about becoming Purple Plain's official photographer then?" Patsy offered.

Trisha did her best to calm herself and forced a smile and an apology. "Not going to happen, I'm afraid. I have too much work on my plate from now until Christmas and I leave Calgary as soon as Stampede is over anyway."

"It was worth a try." Trisha sensed she hadn't heard the last of that offer as Patsy changed the direction of the conversation. "So tell me, what criteria do you use when you judge photos? Lighting, composition and the type of camera the photographer used?"

"All of the above." Thankful for the diversion, Trisha turned her mind to answering the question. Right now her skill as a photographer was one sure thing to hang on to. "The key element every time I look at a photograph is to ask what it does for me. Does it tell me a story? If I get a gut feeling, if that photo grabs my attention in some way, then I'll give it my full consideration even if it breaks all the technical rules."

"I like that you can work outside the box. Not many people think that way" Patsy nodded towards the poster display. "Do you feel that any of these bad boys are rule breakers?"

"Ah, now that would be telling and I still have a week to make up my mind."

Samantha rejoined them, wearing a satisfied grin. For once Trisha didn't want to hear about another Samantha super-deal, or listen to recounted repartee illustrating how sharp and sassy she'd been. She wanted to get outside with her camera and start doing her job, the real reason she had come to Calgary and the Stampede. She picked up her bag and excused herself, telling Samantha she'd call her later.

The heat hit her as she exited the exhibition hall but she didn't let it bother her as she took out her faithful old Fuji camera. It served her purpose well enough for today. She checked her battery strength but before she could refigure the settings someone gently bumped her elbow. She looked up with annoyance only to find Brent Heywood grinning down at her.

"Hello, Ms. Watts. Or should I say howdy?"

His high cheek bones and lean jaw would certainly make any girl look twice, but a hardness that she didn't like lurked in his eyes.

"Hi, Brent. Enjoying yourself?"

"I'd enjoy myself more if I could be sure of your intentions."

Still rattled from her recent shock of seeing Cameron, Trisha was in no mood to have Brent pump her for details.

"Brent," his name hissed like a curse from but between her clenched teeth, "I have not long left Patsy Livingstone. If you remember she is the cover designer for Purple Plain Publishing. I'll tell you the same as I told her. I have a week to make my decision and I have to be seen to be doing that. Now, if you'll excuse me I need to get to work."

"Mind if I tag along and see how a professional photographer works?" He grinned unpleasantly.

"Yes, I do mind. I prefer to work alone."

Brent moved closer and put his mouth to her ear. "Or maybe no one wants to work with you."

In spite of the heat a chill wormed its way along her arms making her shiver. She drew away from him, knowing that Brent Heywood could make her life a living hell if she let him.

Brent tipped his hat to her. "Choose wisely, Ms. Watts. Remember, I have as much opportunity as you to make or break."

She breathed a sigh of relief when he wandered away from her. He hadn't gone far when she saw him lean in to whisper something to a motherly looking woman who laughed out loud as she swiped at his arm. There was no doubt the comment had been racy and in spite of her reaction the woman obviously loved it.

Trisha checked her camera again, screwing her face into a frown as she did so. Anyone seeing her might think she had a problem with a lens or had to adjust the settings. They wouldn't see her inner turmoil. Few people connected Trisha Watts, photographer, with Patricia Somerville, three-day event rider. She liked the anonymity that gave her.

But Brent Heywood could blow that anonymity to smithereens if he so chose. She had worked so hard to put the past behind her. To believe the counselor when he told her it had been an unfortunate accident and not her fault.

How could it not be her fault? She should have pulled Delacourt up when he stumbled but instead she pushed him on. He'd jumped big, and she knew she would have to ask him to lengthen his stride between the two jumps to safely negotiate the second part of the combination. But Delacourt didn't complete the jump, he simply crashed into the ground. She'd been thrown out of the saddle but the momentum of his thousand pound body drove her into the post and rails fence.

She put her hands over her ears to shut out the sounds of that day. The sharp crack like a pistol shot as her head hit a post, then the timber rails splintering as their combined weight demolished the fence, the shocked cries from the crowd. Someone threw a blanket over Delacourt's head, and then she'd passed out.

Trisha blinked back the tears that stung her eyes. Her fault. No one else's. She lived with it every day of her life, hoping and praying that Trisha Watts could bury Patricia Somerville forever. That Brent Heywood had connected the dots meant he'd searched for her on the internet. But now she either had to deal with the truth, however hard that would be, or allow herself to be blackmailed and that she could not do. Hefting the weight of the camera in her hands, Trisha put Brent Heywood out of her mind.

Happy crowds milled around her and the shadows lengthened as Trisha started taking photos of the Saddledome, aptly named for the shape of its roof, at the north end of the Stampede grounds. She snapped pictures of cattle and horses in the Agricultural Barn. Charmed by the sight of a curly-haired moppet asleep at the feet of a massive Clydesdale horse, she asked the mother's permission she take a picture. Several shots later, she exchanged business cards with the mom and promised copies of the photos. Her shots of the kiosks, midway rides and the grandstand would be for general background cover; the real work would start when she began her interviews.

Lively music from the Nashville North tent drew her attention and she flashed her press pass as she made her way to the head of the line to gain entrance. Only a few people grumbled, most were happy to let her by. Once inside she watched the dancers spin their way around the dance floor and thought of two-stepping with

Cameron at the Tumbleweed. She could hardly believe that it had actually happened and envy for the happy couples on the floor niggled its way into her mind.

When she'd taken as many photos as she needed she wandered outside again and headed for the Indian Village at the south end of the grounds. She stopped on the bridge spanning the Elbow River to take a shot of the sun dappled water rippling beneath it. Getting the light right took all her attention and just as she depressed the shutter button her cell phone rang. Intuition told her it would be Cameron.

How did he have the damn nerve? Her bruised ego yelled 'ignore him' but after taking her shot she leaned her elbows on the bridge railing while she reconsidered. The shimmering reflection of the water beneath her almost blinded her and she closed her eyes.

Ignoring him would not resolve anything. It would show her instead as being shallow and immature. But wasn't that what she had already shown him? Being bowled over by his looks and his gentle ways didn't excuse her falling into bed with him. And just why had she allowed that to happen?

Because you couldn't help yourself.
Because you didn't want to help yourself.

The truth of that fact rankled in her mind. Having now recognized her own weakness, there could be only one way to resolve it. One thing she knew for sure, hiding from Cameron would solve nothing, just as he had said. She had to know now where she stood. Had he believed her this morning after all and decided to not wait until Stampede was over before moving on?

She ran a hesitant finger over the face of her phone before finally speed dialing his number. Part of her hoped he wouldn't pick up, part of her hoped to hear his voice. All of her hoped she'd made a mistake.

"Hey, where are you?" He sounded happy and confident.

And why shouldn't he be? He had it all. Two women should be enough for any man to swing between. Or were there more girls out there she knew nothing of? She drew her brows into a deep frown.

"Hey, Trish, are you there?" A note of concern crept into his voice.

Her senses homed in on that concern. Could she believe him? She swallowed her doubt. "I'm at the south end of the grounds on the bridge."

"Stay put, I'll be right over."

She replaced her phone in her bag and wrapped her arms around her middle, uncertain how to face him. She could ask him outright about the girl but wouldn't that be an opening for him to lie? She wanted nothing but the truth now, but how would she recognize it?

She knew he was there an instant before he put his arm around her waist. Damn, why did she have to be so aware of him? She stiffened.

"You don't appear to be in the mood for the Ranchman's," he said, quickly sensing the change in her.

"If you don't mind, I'd rather give it a miss tonight. There's still another week, we could try for another evening." Trisha bit her lip. What was she thinking? She intended to not see him after tonight. Might as well get the hurt over with all at once. "Or not, as you seem to have someone else in your sights."

"Someone else?" Cameron turned her to face him. "What are you talking about?"

"Where were you this afternoon, Cam?"

"Right here in the barns or around the infield all day with the rest of the guys waiting for my go-round. Why would you ask?"

"How did you make out?" She made her voice as casual as she could but her heart thumped uncomfortably as she waited for his reply. Could she have been mistaken? Could two men really look so alike? And come to that, had she really seen the guy's face this afternoon? She'd seen a tall, broad shouldered man wearing a plaid shirt and a black, wide brimmed hat. She'd heard him laugh but she hadn't actually seen his face. She brought her attention back Cameron.

"Nailed it with time in hand," he said. "I'm hoping to keep my lead, but I've got two other guys leasing Anchorman and I have to keep him fresh. Now there's a sport horse for you if ever there was one."

Trisha continued to worry her lip while she considered what he'd said. It didn't make sense. He couldn't have been in two places at once.

"Do you know any long legged blonde girls about my height with a penchant for pink cowboy boots?" she persisted, hating herself for not being able to forget that image.

"Pink cowboy boots?" Cameron shuddered. "If you think that appeals to me, you read me all wrong."

Only slightly reassured, Trisha relaxed a little. It wasn't his last remark that bugged her, but the fact he had been at the rodeo. He couldn't have been in two places at the same time.

"So you didn't go to the Western Art Exhibition today?"

He looked at her with narrowed eyes. "Why am I getting the third degree here? I told you I've been at the rodeo all afternoon."

Trisha looked away from him. Maybe he was right. Maybe she had got it all wrong. Heck, rumor was that everyone had a double somewhere and maybe his had been right here today. She turned to look at him. Confusion warred with query in his steady grey eyes and it cut her like jagged glass to know that she caused it.

"Put it down to lack of sleep and too much excitement. I must have seen someone who looked like you and laughed like you, that's all." Trisha looked away again and fell silent.

"Hey, it happens." Cameron turned her to face him. "So how about a quiet barbeque at my place this evening and you can tell me why you photograph horses but don't ride them?"

In spite of her doubts the small part of her heart that still wanted to trust him dictated that she could not refuse his offer.

* * *

Brent Heywood stepped out from the shade of the lottery booth where he'd been checking out the fancy home first-prize. That stop gave him the opportunity to watch Trisha Watts and her cowboy with them being none the wiser.

He tailed them through the crowds not at all concerned that they might turn and see him. From the way the guy hung his arm around Trisha's shoulders and frequently bent his head towards her, they were too interested in each other to notice him.

From time to time he hung back as they stopped for the big guy to talk to someone or to look at something that caught Trisha's attention. Then he could follow them no further as they passed a security point and crossed the racetrack, heading for the infield grandstand. He watched until they were out of sight. He'd got a good look at the big cowboy attached like Velcro to Trisha's side. A sudden thought prompted by the dust patches on the guy's jeans and shirt sent Brent in search of a program.

Buying one didn't feature in his scheme of things. He wandered through the crowds, looking about for what he needed and smiled with satisfaction when he found it. A group of teenage girls, chattering like monkeys, paid no attention to him as he strolled behind them. One of the girls had trouble keeping the straps of her bag on her shoulder. She hoisted it twice, but still a strap slipped allowing the bag to gape open showing the program lodged there. Brent slid his fingers inside the bag and lifted it without its owner being any the wiser.

He gradually fell back until the girls were out of sight then he found a bench in the sun where he made himself comfortable. He wasn't in the least bit interested in the rodeo events themselves, only the pictures of the contestants.

The way he figured it, a guy had to be crazy to even want to get on any animal that didn't want to be gotten on. He slowly turned the pages, looking at the photographs of the saddle bronc and bareback riders, the bull riders and steer wrestlers. He especially paid attention to the names printed beneath the photos until he found what he'd been looking for. He nodded his head with a satisfied grunt and flicked the page with his forefinger. He liked the finality in the snapping sound of his fingernail hitting the glossy paper.

"Gotcha," he murmured. "Cameron Carter. Now to do some digging on you, buddy, and see just how much of a wrench you can help me throw in your girlfriend's works."

He left the program on the bench, got up and walked away.

Chapter Thirteen

Cameron watched Trisha from the corner of his eye. He'd rather be looking at her full on but needed to keep his eyes on the road. She'd been on edge since he met up with her at the grounds and was still quiet. He didn't know if she believed him or was still mad at him.

Why was she so adamant that she'd seen him? There must be hundreds of six foot plus guys in and around Stampede. The tie-down ropers and steer wrestlers like himself tended to be well built, not like the bronc and bull riders who were often lighter, wiry guys. He'd tried bull riding on a couple of occasions but valued his back too much to follow it through, much to his mom and dad's relief.

What Trisha said about the laugh she heard bothered him some. Only one person could laugh like him, and that person was thousands of miles away. Her concern that he might go for a blonde girl in pink cowboy boots surprised him too. Blonde; somewhere in his past, maybe. Pink boots; definitely not.

They sped along the highway under an indigo sky shot through with layers of pink and orange as the sun dropped behind the craggy mountain peaks. A sudden rush of air in the cab carried on it the heady scent of wolf willow and made him turn his head. Trisha had opened the window and dropped her chin onto her arm where it rested on the frame. He heard her sigh and made no attempt at conversation, hoping the silence would give her time to sort out whatever disturbed her. He couldn't know how her mind argued one way for him, then against him, or that she vibrated with awareness of him the whole time.

She heard him lift his hand from the steering wheel, sensed him turn his head towards her, knew when his gaze fell on her still form.

"Don't you drive better when you're watching the road?" she asked.

"Can't blame a man for looking at the prettiest thing in creation," he cracked back.

"Oh, you were looking at the sunset too? That's even worse."

She heard Cameron's soft chuckle and the sound flowed over her as easily as a ray of sunshine. The truck slowed, she heard the change in the engine tone as the gears dropped when they turned into the driveway.

The sense of coming home, of being in the right place with the right person scared her witless. She didn't even feel like this when she went to her parent's house, the home she had known for most of her life.

As Cameron parked the truck, she sat up and looked across at him, drinking in the outline of his cheek and his slightly shadowed jaw. He turned to look at her and the smile that curved his lips warmed every part of her. She must have been wrong about seeing him in the exhibition hall that afternoon. He couldn't possibly look at her with that gleam of pleasure in his eyes if he was involved with someone else.

Trisha got out of the truck as he swung out of the driver's seat. The dogs rushed to greet her, as happy now with her as they were with their owner. They both flopped on the veranda when she followed Cameron into the house.

"You hungry?" he asked.

"Well, you did mention something about a steak. Or are you now going to starve me?"

"That might make you good and hungry for something else." He shot her a wicked grin as he went to the fridge and peered into it. "Could you rustle up a salad?"

"Oh, I think I could manage that. At least it doesn't require actual cooking."

He took a covered dish out of the fridge. "I put these in to marinate before we left this morning. They should be just about ready. I'll go and fire up the barbeque."

Trisha's brow wrinkled. "I don't remember seeing a barbeque on the veranda when I came in."

"That's because there isn't one." Cameron kissed her nose. "It's out back on the patio. Come on, I'll show you."

He took her out into the garage and opened a door in the back wall that led out onto a paved patio. She tried to orient the space outside with what she knew of the inside layout.

"This is behind your bedroom?" she asked.

"That's right. I figure to cut a door into that wall at some point so I can walk right out here in the morning."

Cameron went to the brick built kitchen area where he set down the dish of steaks on the counter and turned on the gas barbeque. Trisha followed him, taking in the plexi-glass panels screening one side of the patio. Vines wound up and over the open beams above them.

"Are these grapes?" she asked, reaching up to touch the tight black globes hanging over her head.

"They are indeed, although I don't think I'll be making any wine in a hurry. Not sure what to do with them yet."

She dropped into one of the easy chairs beside the fire pit.

"This is gorgeous. Samantha would die for a patio like this."

"There, that's the tone of the evening gone." Cameron grimaced but followed his comment with a soft chuckle.

"Samantha actually has a heart of gold," Trisha told him. "She just doesn't like anyone to know it. She thinks it would interfere with her big, bad boss-lady image."

Trisha hauled herself out of the chair and returned to the kitchen to prepare the salad. Cameron came in and loaded a tray with cutlery, crockery, buns, butter and condiments. When they took the makings of their meal outside,

Trisha set their places at the table while Cameron dropped the steaks on the grill.

"Medium well, if I remember correctly," he said.

"You must have a mind like a steel trap if you can remember that." Trisha looked up through the beams at the darkening sky, marveling at the multitude of stars that would only become brighter as the night deepened.

"Hey, that was only a couple of days ago, how could I forget?" Cameron flipped the sizzling steaks and Trisha wandered over to watch him, bemused by the attention he'd obviously paid her.

"Beer or wine?" he asked as she stopped beside him.

"White wine if you have it, please."

He opened a small fridge at the end of the counter and peered inside. "Sauvignon Blanc or Chardonnay?"

"I'll have the Chardonnay and have to say this is some restaurant." She watched him expertly pull the cork and pour the wine for her as if he'd done it all his life.

"People usually stay over when they come for a training clinic." He handed her the glass and took a beer for himself. "I like to make everyone comfortable and give them a chance to relax after what often is a stressful day, especially for folks who either have problem horses or are just beginners."

"Do you get a lot of them?"

Cameron considered her question while he placed the steaks on plates. "Usually there's a couple every clinic. They often find that owning a horse is a very different ball game to hiring one for a trail ride or riding lesson. The smart ones do something about it."

"And the others?"

"I feel bad for the horses."

They ate in silence and, when they were done, he refused her offer to help clear away the remnants of their meal but watched her as she sat back in her chair and closed her eyes. She obviously needed to relax and here, surrounded by whispering trees and with the open sky above her, he hoped she'd do exactly that.

He picked up the wine bottle and in answer Trisha held her glass out for him to fill it. An owl hooted followed by a long drawn out cry that quavered on the night air. He saw Trisha stiffen, saw the startled look in her eyes.

"Relax," he murmured, hoping that his voice would calm her. He wanted nothing more than to pull her into his arms but he figured she needed her own space for a while. He'd seen her preoccupation on the trip home, sensed her doubt but wanted her to reach her own conclusions. "It's only a coyote, probably be joined by one or two more yet."

As if confirming his statement one howl became two, then a cacophony of voices as more joined in the canine chorus. Trisha tipped her head back against her chair and listened.

The uncanny sound chilled her bare arms and stiffened the short hairs on the back of her neck.

Cameron left his chair and squatted beside hers. "Quite something, huh?"

She looked up and saw the question in his eyes. Trust had nothing to do with the way her body responded and she took his hand when he offered it. He pulled her up to him and folded his arms around her, dropping a kiss on her head, feathering more kisses down her nose until his lips lingered over hers.

The tip of his tongue searched the seam of her mouth and with a deep sigh she invited him in. He cradled the back of her head in one hand, threading his fingers through her hair. He held her close and one kiss became another, sweet and strong and driving all thoughts from her mind. When he did stop, he touched his fingers to her lips to prevent her saying anything and then drew her with him away from the patio.

She couldn't see a path, but knew there must be one as Cameron led her through the stand of trees behind the house. Moon dappled leaves rustled in the night breeze as they passed beneath overhanging boughs and then Trisha heard the soft babble of water.

They emerged from the trees beside a shallow but swift running creek. She watched the rippling water for a moment and then knelt beside it, ignoring the dampness seeping into the knees of her jeans. She held Cameron's hand for balance as she reached over and dabbled her fingers in the water.

"It's cold." She shivered with the chill of it and shook the droplets off her fingers. As bright as diamonds in the moonlight they arced across the stream and fell back into the flow of the current.

"That's because it's fed by mountain runoff," Cameron explained. He kissed her again then pulled her down with him onto the grass beside the creek.

Warmed by the comfort of his arm holding her and sheltered by his body, Trisha lay contentedly beside him, staring up at the night sky. The outline of leaves framed the brilliance of the canopy above her and took her breath away. She had forgotten how bright the stars could be, how dense the extent of the Milky Way. She tracked the steady path of a satellite and smiled when Cameron pointed at a shooting star. The moon rode high and full, its silver light competing with the stars surrounding it.

The coyotes began to howl again and Trisha turned to Cameron. He shifted onto his side and his head came closer to hers, his lips brushed her temple, her cheek, before once more seeking her mouth.

Trisha wound her arms around his neck and pulled him down. Oh Lord, but his hand felt so good as it slid up underneath her shirt. His fingers teased the edge of her bra then pushed it aside for his palm to replace the lace cup. She bit down on her lip to prevent a moan escaping as his thumb began to prescribe a slow, lazy circle around her nipple.

Had he practiced this move on a girl with long blonde hair and pink cowboy boots? Behind her closed eyes she felt a rush of tears.

Don't think of that now.

Cameron shifted and buried his face in the warmth of her belly. She wound her fingers into his thick, dark hair and held on while he teased her belly button with his tongue. That small damp lick of heat set her body on fire as sure as a spark to tinder.

Let him love you, just love him back.

His kisses demanded more and Trisha gave it. She didn't care if her lips would be bruised come morning or if she had the imprint of his fingers on her skin. His heart beat like a trip hammer under her hand and she loved that she had that effect on him. It had been so long since she had loved anybody, knowing that she didn't deserve this most human of emotions. Was she wrong to want it so badly, even if only for a while because, sure as heck, he'd want nothing to do with her when he learnt the truth about her.

And it would, she knew, be a matter of when not if. Damn the internet. He'd only have to plug in her name on any search engine as Brent Heywood must have done and it would give him chapter and verse on the part of her life she so wanted to close.

Cameron trailed his fingers down her stomach and released the button on her jeans. His touch kindled every nerve in her body. When she drew in a sharp breath he slid his hand into the hollow between her waistband and her belly.

"Black or burgundy?" he murmured as he eased her thong aside.

"Neither," she whispered back. "Want to find out?"

"Not yet."

The night absorbed Trisha's every gasp and sigh as they floated away on the breeze. Cameron's fingers slipped lower and she parted her legs to ease his passage. The soft rustle of leaves above her head and the steady rush of water over the creek bed covered the sound of her moans.

She could no longer think as his fingers stroked her slowly and gently. She didn't want to think at all, only feel as a delicious all consuming pressure built between her thighs.

Her lingering doubts slipped away in a haze of heat and wanting as she lifted her hips with increasing urgency while the coyotes yipped and sang at the moon. Their voices rose as surely as the deep need in her body and when their quavering notes tapered away and faded into silence she collapsed, spent, in Cameron's arms.

* * *

Contentment fit Trisha like a second skin as she lay in the warmth of Cameron's bed, his arm heavy across her waist.

He'd said nothing last night as he'd adjusted her clothes then silently walked her back to the house and straight to his bedroom. He'd kissed her again, slowly stripped her and taken her to bed. The only sound he'd uttered was a soft shush when she would have spoken.

She took her time opening her eyes to a room filled with morning light. The deep veranda roof prevented sunshine streaming in any further than the floor just inside the door.

Cameron's steady breathing told her he still slept and she did not want to disturb him, so lay there in perfect peace matching her breath to his.

She had no idea of the time, nor did she care. She simply relished being with him. For the first time in she couldn't remember how long, a night passed without her sleep being disturbed by dreams. If she had dreamt, she had no recollection of it.

Cameron's arm tightened and he pulled her against him, evidence that he was waking firm against her bare buttocks. She turned to him in lazy delight, twining her arms about his neck and reaching to kiss his still closed eyes.

He lifted her on top of him and she took her time loving him until the smile on his mouth told her he was fully awake. She kissed his face, his mouth, his neck while he guided her hips with his strong hands. Their breath shortened to quick, hard gasps yet neither spoke as their day started with complete and utter satisfaction.

Trisha lay against him, loving the peace in their silence, not wanting to move or to have this moment end. Then Cameron scooted out of bed and strode naked down the hallway, leaving her in the rumpled cocoon of their love makeing. She pulled the sheets over her head to block out the sounds of cupboard doors opening and closing, the rattle of crockery and the buzz of the coffee grinder but when he came and stood beside the bed she knew she had to get up.

He'd already pulled on a pair of clean jeans but held out his robe for her. She shrugged it over her shoulders and fastened the belt around her waist but it wasn't until she once more sat on the veranda with Groucho on one side of her and Busby on the other that he smiled at her and whispered 'good morning'.

She couldn't stop the smile from spreading across her face as she took a mug of coffee from him. "Thank you."

"You're welcome." He raised his mug in a salute to her and then sat back in his own chair.

She had no wish to break the magic of the moment but knew it would soon have to come to an end. It wouldn't be long before he would want to be on the road to head back to Calgary. She heard him sigh and turned her head to watch him stretch out his long legs.

"Do we have to go soon?" she asked.

"Soon enough." He stood up and stretched. "I've got a couple of horses to see to here then we'll have breakfast."

Trisha nodded, in no hurry to offer to cook pancakes and eggs when she knew he could do it more quickly and fix a better meal than she could. She showered and dressed and with still wet hair waited for him on the veranda. The dogs had gone and she supposed they were with him. She wandered over to the barn but found it empty and quiet.

He hadn't said the horses were in there, only that he had to see to them. She stood in the doorway, looking down the driveway and across the corral. There was no sign of him and for a moment she thought she'd entered some kind of time warp. But then a movement in the tree covered slope behind the corral caught her attention.

Her heart leapt at the sight of a pretty grey mare with a long-legged black foal alongside. She remembered another grey mare and another black foal, but pushed that painful memory aside and concentrated on Cameron instead. He rode the mare without saddle or bridle, and simply let her pick her way. The foal pranced ahead, then dodged between the slim trunks but rushed to its mother's side again when they left the shelter of the trees.

Cameron wore nothing more than his hat, jeans and boots. Sunlight gilded the dusting of hair on his bare, broad chest and her mouth dried at the sight as she watched him ride towards her.

"You know each other pretty well," she said as he halted the mare beside her.

"Rosie's home bred so I've known her all her life." He drew his leg over the mare's neck and slid off her back. "Her baby is just four months old now. She's a registered quarter horse with the fancy title of Cash's Dream Girl, but for now she's my Sweetpea."

Shy but curious the foal nibbled Trisha's fingers when she held out her hand, making her laugh. "Do you mind if I take some pictures?"

"Be my guest." Cameron draped his arm comfortably across the mare's hindquarters.

Not wanting to miss the best of the morning light, Trisha hurried to fetch her camera then squinted up at the sun to determine where the shadows fell and where would be her best vantage point. The mare watched her with mild curiosity from liquid-dark eyes as Trisha repeatedly snapped the shutter button, dropping to her knee for one shot or squatting down for another to make the most of angles and distance. At last she stopped and reviewed her shots. Cameron came and looked over her shoulder.

"Damn, you are good," he said admiringly as he watched her photos fill the viewing panel. In one shot she'd caught the full, dark globe of Rosie's eye fringed by her long white eyelashes. In another she'd captured the delicate flare of Sweetpea's nostrils. "These aren't even posed."

"No, but if they were I'd have arranged a very different set up."

"How would you do that?"

"For a start," she explained, "I'd have you stand Rosie square on that level patch of gravel there, so I could see her feet clearly. I'd have you remove that baler twine from the fence, and move those buckets by the gate out of the way. I want to see the horse, not what's around it and

I'd use my Canon as it has a higher shutter speed."

Cameron laughed. "Now that kind of talk is as foreign to me as you say riding is to you." He leaned in and planted a kiss on her cheek.

Trisha nodded, not trusting herself to speak. His comment made her think she'd somehow given herself away. Or had Brent already set something in motion? Her doubts from yesterday swirled to the surface. In spite of the sunshine she shivered as Cameron gently hazed Rosie and Sweetpea into the corral. Rosie hung her head over the fence and Sweetpea reached up to nuzzle Cameron's elbow as he leaned it on the top rail. She took one more photograph of the three of them.

It might be all she had to remember him by.

Chapter Fourteen

"You're like a damn genie in a bottle," Samantha grumbled as they sat in her office. "Here one minute then poof, gone the next. Do I get brownie points for guessing where you were?"

Trisha chuckled. "No, you don't. And stop complaining. If I'm not here half the time it's your fault for having connived to get Cameron to take me trail riding."

"Ah, the god in blue jeans. How is he?"

"Very well, thank you."

"You're still not going to tell me anything?"

"Nope."

"You are so mean." Samantha set down a stack of manila folders on her desk. "I'm aquiver with anticipation over your love life because mine sucks. Although, I must say you look very much better than the pale and pasty waif I picked up at the airport. I think you've put on a pound or two as well."

"Really? Where?" Trisha looked down at her still slim figure. "And for the record, you didn't pick me up. Dee did."

"Oh, well," Samantha hesitated with a frown on her face. "I meant to."

"She said you were having trouble with some girl over a contract."

"I'm always having trouble with contracts. Look at these."

Trisha picked up the top folder from the pile Samantha pushed towards her and leafed through it, surprised at the number of crossings out and hand-written side notes on the forms.

"Everyone and his dog has a lawyer these days," Samantha continued. "Lord knows I'm a very patient person but this is enough to drive a saint crazy."

"Patient? You?" Trisha raised an eyebrow. "Even on your best day, patience is not one of your virtues."

She continued to flip through the folders. Some of the demands were not unreasonable, others outrageous. A soft whirring sound made her look up in time to see sunscreens rolling down the windows.

"Sensors," Samantha explained. "They're a god-send. Saves me a lot of time adjusting the blinds."

"All of six seconds I'm sure," Trisha teased.

Samantha made a face at her then looked up as Marguerite DeVries walked in.

"You called, I came." Marguerite waved an imperious hand as she sank into a chair. "Oh, and I brought more photos of our models. I thought they might help Trisha pick her winner although I must say they all give me hot flashes and I'm not even menopausal."

She fanned her face as if to cool it off with a large, bulky envelope.

Samantha took it from her and laid it on the desk. "What we have to tell you might give you a hot flash of another variety."

Marguerite raised an eyebrow as she looked at Samantha, than swiveled her chair and glanced at Trisha.

"What's going on here? Should I be worried?"

"Possibly." Samantha fidgeted with the edge of the envelope. "I may have been a bit hasty in putting Trisha's name forward as your judge."

"It wouldn't have been hasty had she told me exactly what she'd let me in for," Trisha began hesitantly, still angry with Samantha but not wanting to start a blame game. "I'm sorry, Marguerite, had I known what was involved I'd have refused the offer because I'm best known for taking photos of horses, not people."

"I noticed you with a little group on Friday night. Samantha said they were friends of yours." Marguerite gave her a calculating glare. "Was that guy you were with trying to influence you to pick his friend for first place?"

"No, he wasn't." Trisha rubbed her clammy palms down her thighs, drying them on her jeans. She had to avert any suspicious thoughts Marguerite might have about Cameron. "But someone else is."

"Who?" Marguerite demanded.

"Brent Heywood," she admitted. "Believe me, it would be far better if I simply fade out of the picture. You can say I was sick or something. I know it's far from professional but you don't want Brent Heywood mouthing off about me. It would create bad press and question the validity of your event."

"Whoa. Just a minute, lady." Marguerite pushed her chair back, got to her feet and strode to the window and back. "That's a lot to hit me with the now the event is underway. What gives?"

Somewhere in the recesses of her mind and quite illogically Trisha registered an eight-second time frame for Marguerite to walk to and from the window. Maybe those automatic sunscreens were worth it after all.

"What's Brent Heywood got on you?" Marguerite angled her head to one side, her eyes gleaming with sharp interest as she looked at Trisha.

Tears pricked Trisha's eyes. However much she wanted to put her past behind her, here it was yet again staring in her in the face. For how much longer could she run from the truth of a day she wished she could forget? She put her hand over her mouth to choke a sob. She was so sick and tired of feeling weak and afraid yet still could not find the words to explain herself.

"Something happened to me a couple of years ago. Something I'm still trying to get past. I'm sorry but I really don't want to talk about it." Trisha turned away, misery pulling her mouth down.

"And it's plain eating her up, that's why she's so skinny," Samantha cut in. "But if a smarm like Brent Heywood could uncover information about you, Trisha, then so could anyone with a computer and half a brain."

"If he's really being that much of a pest we'll just find grounds to disqualify him," Marguerite snorted.

"You can't do that, Marguerite," Trisha warned. "Forgive the analogy but he's got a loaded gun here. Either I give him what he wants, which is to win the prize pot, the cover shoot and the contract deal, or he will bad mouth me to everyone who will listen. It would be totally unfair to the other competitors for me to give in to his demands and Samantha's and your integrity will be compromised if I do. Both of you have too much to lose for me to allow that to happen."

"But if you back out now, what's to stop him talking anyway? He could put his own spin on it just to get back at you. I can see it now." Samantha held her hands up as if framing a tabloid headline. "'Judge walks out on top publishing house'. You think the fallout from that wouldn't have some effect?"

"Has he tried to contact you again?" Marguerite asked.

"No, thank goodness," Trisha admitted. "But this is only Sunday. We've still got six days to go before the winner is announced. I can't think of anything we could do to make this right."

"I can." Marguerite grinned suddenly. "Honey, if you're up for this we can absolutely turn it around. But it might mean an uncomfortable week for you."

Fear of what Brent Heywood might do and what solution Marguerite may have vied in Trisha's mind.

"What could you do?" she asked finally.

In answer Marguerite reached into her voluminous designer bag, sifted through its contents and retrieved a piece of paper. "This is our Pick-a-Dinner-Date draw form. This is what we were going to run with in the first place, and then Samantha thought we'd get more exposure with you judging the finals. You do have the credentials, you know. I checked that much."

Trisha took the draw form and quickly scanned it. The only information asked for was the entrant's name, email address and with which model they would most like to have dinner.

"So you really didn't need me anyway." Trisha glared at Samantha.

"You give the event that professional edge we needed." Samantha did not look at all repentant. "All the draw forms will have to be processed anyway. Marguerite has a team of Purple Plain readers ready to start work on them, if they haven't already."

"That begins tomorrow morning at nine," Marguerite added. "We didn't know what the response would be like but it's already astronomical. I guess everyone wants a date with a winning male model, and a few of them are real cowboys. Now we have our work cut out to get everything counted by four o'clock on Saturday afternoon ready for the evening announcement. Our part of the exhibition is over at midnight Friday when our photo display comes down."

Trisha waved the draw form under Marguerite's nose. "There will be thousands of these. How can you possibly process them all in less than a week?"

"Never underestimate the power of our readers," Marguerite chuckled. "If you don't have plans tomorrow, meet me at my office and I'll show you what I mean."

Intrigued in spite of her initial doubt, Trisha agreed. "So what should I do about Brent?"

"He's not stalking you, is he?" Marguerite asked with friendly concern. "He hasn't actually threatened you with physical harm?"

"No." Trisha shivered at the thought. His bumping into her at the Stampede grounds was nothing more than a coincidence. It couldn't be anything else, could it?

"If he approaches you again just let him think he's convinced you to pick him. What do you think, Samantha?"

Samantha tapped a nail against her cheek as she considered. "I think we need to find out more about him. I'll have Dee look into his background. She has ways and means I don't even want to think about."

"The stage manager from Friday night didn't have a very good opinion of him either," Trisha said. "I'll see if I can track him down and ask him what he meant. I was too upset to think straight then. I just wanted to leave."

"I can understand that." Samantha threw her arm around Trisha's shoulders and gave her a quick, comforting squeeze. "I'll have Dee call him first; she liaised with him for the reception and awards night at the Palliser so she'll have his number."

Trisha covered her face with her hands and shook her head. "I thought coming here would be a bit of a vacation along with my assignment. Instead, my past is catching up with me almost faster than I can breathe."

"What could have been so bad?" Marguerite wanted to know.

"Stampede and horses go together. Cowboys and horses go together. Your judge and a dead horse don't, but that's what will come out of this if I don't give in to Brent Heywood's demands."

"I think you should tell us what happened," Marguerite advised. "Whatever it is, let us help you deal with it."

Trisha looked at both women but heard her counselor's voice.

There will come a time, Trisha, when you become so tired of the burden of guilt you've chosen to carry. Then your only options will be to either sink under its weight or swim away from it. Sink or swim. It's up to you.

Trisha straightened her back and shoulders, lifted her chin. She'd carried that guilt for two years. She'd lain down with it at night, an uncomfortable and unforgiving bed-fellow and gotten up with it in the morning after dream-disturbed sleep. It sapped her energy and drained all emotion leaving her living a half-life.

Sink or swim. More of what she had suffered in the last two years? No.

Trisha looked at Samantha and Marguerite, saw the tension in their faces and the questions in their eyes. Where should she begin? With her parents who had her on a horse before she could walk? With Delacourt, the horse bred by her mother and trained by her father? With her own soul-deep passion for horses? Simply with herself? It all seemed too much. She sank into the nearest chair.

"Before I became Trisha Watts, photographer, I was Patricia Somerville, three-day event rider. In our last event in the run up for the European championships, my horse stumbled and I ignored it and pushed him on over a jump. He was dead when he hit the ground and we finished up crashing into another fence. I hit my head and was in a coma for eight weeks." Trisha reached up and pushed back her bangs, revealing the scar on her forehead.

"Ouch," muttered Samantha.

"Ouch is right, on so many levels," Trisha continued. "When the hospital finally discharged me and I went home, I found I'd not only lost my sense of balance and some depth perception, but also my nerve. I couldn't get on a horse without breaking out in a cold sweat and having nightmares afterwards. My parents thought I just needed to persist but it simply got worse until I had a huge argument with my father and left home to stay with a friend. I couldn't get on a horse but I could still photograph them so made photography my career."

On the edge of tears, Trisha's voice quavered and she stopped.

"Did you know any of this?" Marguerite asked Samantha.

"Some of it," Samantha admitted, "but I thought it best for Trish to tell you herself."

"All Samantha knew of me when we met in Toronto," Trisha continued, "was that a designer had asked me to be one of his models. He knew that I rode in top level competition and thought my name might help advertise his riding inspired fashions. When I refused to model he asked me to shoot at fashion week instead because he'd also seen an exhibition of my photographs in a London art gallery."

"So the name Watts is a pseudonym?" Marguerite wanted to know.

"No, that's my mother's maiden name."

"Well, your story could be a novel all on its own," Marguerite mused.

"So now you know the truth, do you really want to risk all that coming out in the press right now?" Trisha worried at her lower lip.

"Actually, yes." Samantha suddenly smiled and held up her hand as Trisha began to protest. "I know several journalists and one in particular would be very sympathetic. Trisha, think about it. It gives you an opportunity to show how brave you are in admitting the problem you had and why you turned to photography. How many other people might be out there suffering the way you do? Your story might help them and stop Brent Heywood in his tracks too."

"That could work." Marguerite looked thoughtful while she considered Samantha's proposal. "What do you think, Trisha? Are you up for it?"

Trisha looked at the women who were for now her closest colleagues. Having gone this far, it would be impossible for her to not help make their event a success. And did she really want the man who made her skin crawl just to think of him gain the upper hand? She slowly nodded her assent.

"Okay, set up the interview. Let's get it over with."

Chapter Fifteen

It took no time at all for Brent Heywood to discover the location of Samantha Monroe's home address. Checking out her condo this morning, he'd watched her and Patricia—he couldn't think of her as Trisha—emerge onto the sidewalk. He kept his distance but knew they were too busy talking to notice him. As soon as they turned onto Fourth Avenue he realized they must be heading for Samantha's office. They entered her tower building and he pushed through the entrance in time to see the elevator doors close behind them.

He checked the directory to make sure he knew what floor they were on. He'd need it soon anyway as he'd probably be going there himself to sign a contract. As he turned away from it he came face to face with a security guard hovering on the edge of suspicion. Narrowed eyes, lips pressed firmly together, arms crossed over his chest. Brent knew the signs well

"Can I help you?" the guard asked.

Brent smiled easily. He couldn't think what he'd done to attract the guard's attention but refused to be intimidated. "Just checking out an address for an appointment tomorrow. I don't want to be late."

"Hm." The guard didn't sound convinced.

Spotting a convenience kiosk Brent offered to get him a coffee but the guard shook his head. Brent had no idea how long he would have to wait before Samantha and Patricia showed up again. He didn't want the guard hanging around him nor did he want to leave yet so bought a coffee and a Sunday newspaper. He might just as well make himself comfortable and soon found a seat from where he could see both the entrance and the elevator.

When Marguerite DeVries arrived he supposed they must be having a meeting about the competition. A second coffee went cold before the elevator doors opened and the three women came out together. As they left the building he went to stand by the lobby window and watched them pile into a taxi waiting at the curb.

They were probably going to the Stampede grounds. He thought of the hundred dollar bill folded in his wallet. Nope. No point even thinking of following them. Discovering Patricia's skeleton in the closet had been more than a stroke of luck, it assured him a $25,000 payday come Saturday. He could feel the check in his hand and see the dates for modeling shoots filling his calendar. Once he'd got a cover or two under his belt he'd turn himself into his own business.

Thinking about how he'd manage that occupied him as he made his way back to the motel. There'd be no more messing around with trains, taxis and buses. Oh, no. He knew exactly which vehicle would suit him and then he'd travel in style.

Once in his room he stripped to the waist for comfort and sat on the bed. Marginally better than his usual accommodation, at least it had air conditioning and the beer he'd pulled out of the fridge chilled his hand.

He opened up his laptop and reviewed the information he'd found earlier that day, considering how best to use it. What did Patricia really know about Carter? He didn't think they could have had much time together as she'd only been in town such a short time, but judging from what he'd seen so far he figured they didn't get much talking done.

Did she know that Cameron Carter had a brother? That they had competed in rodeo as partners since their early teens? He thought not but couldn't be sure. Taking another pull on his beer, he tapped a key and brought up a picture of Cameron and Mackenzie Carter.

"Hot damn," he muttered as he scrutinized the picture. Then he began to chuckle. "Well, well. This could be mighty useful."

Setting the beer on the nightstand, he began to type in earnest. On a whim he brought up the online telephone directory for Calgary, just in case either brother had a land-line listed. Disappointed but not surprised when he didn't find one, he went back to scrolling through the Canadian rodeo listings. The brothers' names cropped up consistently then suddenly disappeared. What happened?

He carried on searching and then found Cameron's name again, but not Mackenzie's. Maybe they'd argued, not an unheard of occurrence between competitive brothers, or so he understood. Having no siblings of his own, he had no first-hand experience. He typed Mackenzie Carter in the search bar and groaned as both male and female listings appeared on the screen with not a rodeo performer amongst them.

He finished his beer and stared at the bottle in moody silence. He'd like another but considered his finances and knew he'd have to make this six-pack last a few days. His last job had been managing a gym. It had paid more than just his bi-weekly pay check. He grinned as he remembered flirting with cute young women as he took or renewed their memberships but he'd gone much further than flirting with several of the hard-bodied, bored businessmen's wives he'd met. A photograph here and a quiet word there had cash pouring into his pockets. This he'd stashed in a small storage unit. He'd rented it to hide things he hadn't wanted his mother to see but gave it up when she passed away.

For once it didn't irritate him that his only inheritance from her was the good looks he'd been born with. While he'd worked at the gym he'd kept himself fit. It had been one of his interests who had suggested he enter the cover model competition. He'd paid a small fortune for his portfolio of photographs but didn't regret it now that he had something to look forward to.

He'd never be like his mother who'd worked two and sometimes three jobs to keep a roof over their heads. In between those jobs there'd been a succession of 'uncles', mostly itinerant workers who used her and their home for a month or two and then were gone. Some taught him useful tricks, like stacking a deck of cards in his favor or the easiest way to lift a wallet.

He sighed and heaved himself off the bed. Once he'd showered and freshened up he'd head out for the evening.

..*

The sun sat low in the dusk-hazed sky, a mere beat away from sliding behind the backdrop of the shadow darkened mountains. Despite the late hour, heat still drilled down on rooftops, bathed tall buildings in a rosy glow and drove people into the bars along Seventeenth Avenue which drew Brent like beacons.

Timing is everything, one of his uncles once advised him. Go into a bar too early when the crowd is thin and people are likely to remember you. Wait until later when it's noisy and folks are buzzed then you just become a blur in the crowd.

He considered the wisdom of that advice as he scanned a party crowd. They spilled out from a pub's dim interior onto the sidewalk patio but he ignored them as he spotted something infinitely more attractive and elbowed his way to the bar.

His eyes fixed on the sweet curve of the girl's Daisy-Dukes clad butt as she leaned across the bar to speak to a barman. Her shapely bare legs ended in a pair of pink, tooled leather cowboy boots. Cute. He moved closer as she flicked her long blonde hair over her shoulder, saw the barman place two glasses of beer in front of her. Shit. Did that mean she had a date?

He hit the bar at the same time she turned to leave it. He smiled but knew he barely registered on her radar as her blue eyes lit up at something behind him. He half turned, saw who she met and quickly faced the bar again.

"Hey, buddy." The barman watched him with ill-disguised impatience. "Are you droolin' or drinkin'?"

Brent ordered his usual beer and whiskey chaser and made his way to the edge of the party crowd but before he got there someone plucked at his sleeve. He looked down at the turquoise-tipped fingers on his arm, then at their owner.

"We have room at our table if you'd like to join us," she offered, batting her eyelashes at him.

He looked at her and her two companions as if considering, but then he remembered his mother attaching false eyelashes before a night on the town. The recollection made him falter but he quickly recovered himself and smiled, recognizing the faint hope in this woman's eyes. At the very least she'd likely buy him a drink, possibly supper. He nodded and sat in the chair beside her while she introduced herself as Connie and her companions as Joyce and Diane.

"With pleasure, ladies." He tipped his hat to them, aware that Diane studied him carefully.

"You're one of those cover models," she suddenly announced. "I saw your picture in the Exhibition Centre at the Stampede."

Connie and Joyce looked at him as closely as had Diane. Then they started to chuckle. For a moment Brent felt unusually uncomfortable but then he grinned and swept off his hat.

"You got me pegged right, ladies." He smiled at them while he held the hat over his heart before settling it on his head again.

"Are we talking to the winner?" Connie asked coyly.

Brent shook his head. "I have it on the best authority that the judge has until the end of the week to make her decision. The winner will be announced Saturday night. I'm hopeful, but it's a tough line up."

"I certainly wouldn't want to be that judge," Diane chimed in. "How could anyone make a decision from all those gorgeous men?"

Brent leaned in to her and lowered his voice. "Are you calling me gorgeous?"

"Well, you are." Connie's giggle told him that she'd had more than a few drinks.

"Well, thank you, ma'am." He raised his hat to her and sat back in his chair as Diane beckoned the waitress over and ordered drinks for them all.

"Now, hang on a minute Diane." Brent motioned the waitress to wait. "I can't accept your hospitality without—"

"Don't be silly. Of course you can," Diane said. The waitress scurried away before anyone could change their mind.

Connie stared at him for so long he was certain she was trying to focus her vision.

"So do you get your good looks from your mom or your dad?" she asked.

He blew out a breath and arranged his features to look grim. "Never knew who my father was, I'm sad to say. My mom was the looker."

"Was?" Connie stroked the back of his hand as if to commiserate.

"She passed away last year." Brent bowed his head. Respect for his mother was sure to raise him in these ladies' esteem.

"That must have been tough for you. Have you any brothers or sisters?"

Brent shook his head, pressed his lips together and closed his eyes as if the subject was too painful for him. "None."

"That is so sad." Connie grabbed his hand and gave it a comforting squeeze. Brent retrieved it and gave her a shy smile.

Joyce leaned towards him then, raising her voice to make sure he could hear her above the din in the pub. "Tell us what it's like being a model."

Brent sat back in his chair, a warm glow of well-being spreading in his stomach. He had the ladies in the palms of his hands. He entertained them with tales about photo shoots, both real and imagined, and had them almost crying in their drinks as he described his first attempts at waxing his chest.

Between the booze and the laughter he hadn't failed to keep an eye on Carter and the blonde girl. When it looked as if they were making a move to leave, he got to his feet.

"Come on ladies," he coaxed. "Time for a group photo. Connie, move in closer to Diane and Joyce. Just one photo to celebrate a good night out. That's it. Lovely."

He had to grit his teeth when Connie snatched his hat and put it on her head. He smiled anyway and purposely focused his phone slightly above them. He took two shots and quickly viewed them, then held his hand over his face and groaned.

"Ladies, I am so bad. I've got nothing but the tops of your lovely heads. Let me take one more." He snapped the photograph he could have taken in the first place and showed it to them, promising he'd send it to them as they pressed a napkin covered with their email addresses into his hand. 'Well, ladies, sad to say I'm going to have to leave you. It's not just the girls who need their beauty sleep you know."

He went around the table and thanked each of them for a fun and entertaining evening. They giggled like schoolgirls when he kissed their cheeks and Connie goosed him when he retrieved his hat. He wagged his finger at her but by then he doubted she could even see it. In the pool of light outside the door he stopped and quickly looked at the photos he'd just taken.

They were clean, clear shots and no one could mistake the couple in the pictures because there, front and center, were Carter and his girlfriend.

Chapter Sixteen

How could it be Monday already?

Trisha glared at the clock then turned on her back and stared at the ceiling, irritated with herself for missing the warm weight of Cameron's body curled around hers and the soft rasp of his breathing in her ear. She turned her face into the pillow with a groan. She'd known Cameron Carter for all of a week. No, make that six days. The skin on her shoulder where he'd touched her that first day still seemed to burn, as if he'd branded her. Whether it was a hot or a cold brand, to her either denoted ownership. She didn't want to be owned, but she did want to be with Cameron.

Was that why she'd tumbled into bed with him at the earliest opportunity? And if so, what did that make her? Never mind that he'd kicked her libido into overdrive, leaving her floating on a cloud that she didn't want to get off. It had to be lust because the alternative was unthinkable. He was an almighty itch that she wanted to scratch and she'd done just that so might be over him already. But, from the way her body surged into demanding life just thinking about him, she knew that was one big, fat lie.

Her thoughts were rudely interrupted by Samantha banging on her door.

"We're due at Marguerite's in an hour," she yelled.

Trisha wriggled out of bed. "I'm not deaf."

"Didn't think you were," Samantha shouted back. "Just wanted to make sure you were up."

"In more ways than you can imagine," Trisha muttered angrily as she walked into the bathroom and turned on the shower.

Cameron still filled her mind as she and Samantha entered Purple Plain's premises an hour and a half later. Marguerite stood at the reception desk sorting through a bundle of mail. She pulled out a large manila envelope with a smile.

"I've got some more photographs for you Trisha," Marguerite handed her the envelope. "Have you looked at the last lot?"

Trisha nodded. "They are very good. I take it you made your final selection from your original entries and then set up those models with your photographer?"

"Exactly right. Some took direction better than others and I think it shows, but would you like to come and see how we're getting on with tallying the draw tickets? We're in temporary accommodation down the hall." Marguerite took them out of her office and along the main hallway to the next suite.

Even from outside the door Trisha could hear the hum of conversation broken by frequent bursts of laughter. When Marguerite took them inside the din almost deafened her and she looked in astonishment at all the activity. The same poster-size photographs as those on display at the Stampede but with the contestants names clearly printed on the bottom of each of them decorated the walls. A boardroom-sized table, its top covered with neat stacks of draw tickets, had been set up down the center of the room. At each of the twelve workstations around it, sorters with flying fingers worked their way through the tickets.

"If it's any consolation to you Trisha," Marguerite said with a grin, "Brent Heywood is not the most popular pick. So far he's lying in about seventh place."

"And the week has only just begun," added Samantha. "He could come in last by the time we are done. When do entries close?"

"Eleven o'clock on Friday night." Marguerite told them. "We offered the ladies either a night shift or an early start Saturday morning. Several have opted for the night shift so I think our count will be done well before lunch. Then we'll have plenty of time before the reveal and presentations at the Palliser at four."

"I'm impressed." How the sorters could converse and laugh together and not lose track of which pile belonged to which entrant amazed Trisha.

"I told you our readers are awesome." Marguerite nodded towards the table. "They each have a box of tickets and sort them into name order on the table. The four ladies walking around pick up the sorted names and then count them into bundles of one hundred which is easier for the ladies doing the data entry."

"And the majority wins." Trisha said.

Marguerite nodded. "Have you heard any more from Heywood?"

"No, he doesn't have my cell number thank goodness, but that doesn't mean he won't show up beside me when I least expect him," Trisha replied with a shudder. "Even just looking at his picture here makes me uncomfortable."

She looked up at the poster again, as if drawn to it. Brent's straight nose and high cheek bones above a lean jaw were certainly photogenic, but she remembered the coldness in his pale blue eyes and shivered. That icy disregard seemed to follow every move she made yet it could be nothing more than her over-active imagination.

Having seen enough of Marguerite's enterprise, Trisha relaxed a little when they all returned to the main office. She picked up the envelope of photographs she'd been given, opened it and laid them out on Marguerite's desk top.

All the photographs were in black and white, the models mostly bare-chested or wearing unbuttoned shirts. They all had impressive, muscular bodies. In each picture the subject had his head tilted just enough to peer out from beneath the brim of his cowboy hat. Some of them looked a little uncomfortable and Trisha decided these were probably the real cowboys that Marguerite had mentioned. The rest of them showed some degree of comfort with the camera. She couldn't even deny the total confidence she saw in Brent's photograph but looking at it still unsettled her.

Picking all the photographs up in no particular order she shuffled them like a pack of large cards then laid them one by one face down on the table. She picked them up one at a time, looking at each one now as an individual. When all twelve were face up again, she stepped back from the desk but looked up when Marguerite chuckled.

"What?" Trisha tried to look bewildered.

Marguerite stabbed a finger at one particular photo. "From the look on your face and the fact that you've concentrated on that particular photograph twice now, I think you've made your choice."

"My, my." Samantha looked where Marguerite pointed. "That's no surprise. Number Five, Jason Creevey. Why him?"

"I didn't say it was him." Trisha gathered up the photos and replaced them in the envelope. "But I do wonder how he managed to be the only naked guy amongst them. It would seem to give him an unfair advantage."

"We didn't stipulate any dress code in the entry forms," Marguerite said. "I don't think any of us even thought someone would submit a nude photo of themselves. But I don't blame you in the least for picking him. He's definitely book cover material."

"You both told me I had until the end of the week to make a decision so you'll just have to wait and see who I do pick," Trisha said with a grin. "But now you'll have to excuse me. I have to get down to the grounds to start my interviews. I made some contacts before I arrived, but Cameron helped me with some introductions and I'm meeting a stock contractor and a couple of wagon drivers this afternoon."

"Do you want me to come with you?" Samantha asked.

Trisha looked at the stricken expression on her friend's face and laughed. "I don't think so. I just need to go back to the condo to get my gear because I'll be staying for the wagon races tonight."

"And I probably won't see you for days," Samantha grumbled. Her cell phone warbled in her pocket and she pulled it out. "It's Dee," she mouthed as she listened to her assistant. When the call ended she smiled at Trisha. "Your interview is set up for Thursday afternoon at my office. Think you're ready for it?"

"As ready as I'll ever be, I suppose." Trisha caught her lip and turned away.

Darn it, why did the tears have to spring so easily? She couldn't complain even though the mere thought of unburdening herself to a fellow journalist, however sympathetic, terrified her. She had only agreed to the interview to foil Brent Heywood's demands and to change her mind now would simply be playing into his hands.

She must have had a real moment of weakness in agreeing to tell her story. After holding so much so close for so long she could not turn back now.

* * *

"There's the horrrnn annnnnnd theeeeeey're off!"

Drivers yelled and whistled at their horses and the wagons shot forward off their starting barrels. The outriders tossed barrels representing old cook stoves along with two tent poles, into their wagon beds then vaulted on to their own mounts. They sped after the wagons as they made their figure of eight turns around the second marker barrels and out onto the racetrack.

Breathless, Trisha watched the four wagons race round the first bend, their outriders spread across the track behind them. She'd had the finer points of chuck wagon racing explained to her that afternoon by the driver she'd interviewed, but had not been prepared for the noise and speed of it, the rush of adrenaline that surged through her as the horses hit their stride.

A stride that could be twenty feet in length with up to one hundred and fifty strides per minute. An acceleration speed of almost forty-two miles per hour in two-point-five seconds, powered by a heart as big as a basketball and capable of pumping seventy-five gallons of blood every minute. Those facts were ingrained in her by her father from the moment she had sat on her first thoroughbred.

She watched the teams now, all straining into their collars, surging around the track with their hooves pounding the dirt like pistons. The jingle of their harness, the rattle of the wagons and the rumble of the wheels filled her ears as they rounded the final turn. The drivers leaned forward from their seats, slapping the lines on the horses' backs, all of them yelling encouragement to their teams to find that final turn of speed down the homestretch.

"An-n-n-nd Riley Bachmann is at the front of the pack leading the dash for cash, ladies and gentleman. Here he comes now heading to the wire with his wheels on fire. Riley is first across the line with Bart Coleman a horse length behind him in second place."

Some twenty thousand voices erupted in cheers and applause, a wall of noise which blasted Trisha's ears. She watched the teams slowing down to a lope then a trot, all under the control of their drivers again.

Her heart still pounded as she opened her camera bag.

"If you've never seen chuck wagon racing before," another photographer had advised her, "Be sure to watch the first race."

Now she appreciated that advice. Without knowing what to expect she would have had no clear idea of what shots she wanted. She set herself up amongst other photographers at the first then the last turns before crossing to the backstretch so she could catch the action there. From time to time she checked her shots, pleased with her results in capturing the grace and athleticism of the thoroughbreds, the speed and color of the event that ran every day of the Stampede. But the final choice of what would appear in the magazine would be her editor's choice, not hers. It would certainly not be an easy task for him.

With all the race heats run and the teams heading to their barns, she made her way back up into the grandstand to find a suitable place to take pictures of the late night show. Dust clung to her face and clothes and beneath her shirt her cotton tee stuck to her back. Right now she considered herself fortunate to be alone. Sweaty, dusty, she'd hardly make anyone's girlfriend of the year list.

She took several shots of the show stage being set up in front of the grandstand but pictures of the chuck wagons played across her mind. The thrill of those surging bay, brown, grey, black bodies hurtling around that track excited her beyond anything she'd expected. Adrenaline had pumped through her veins as she watched heat after heat, leaving her as breathless as if she'd been up there on the box with a driver or on the back of one of the horses.

Wait.

On the back of one of those horses?

Shocked that she could even have thought it, she let out a slow controlled breath. She'd vowed never to get on a horse again, to never be in the position of risking another horse's life. Yet today, for the first time since her accident, she wanted to feel the wind on her face and in her hair, wanted to experience again that speed and strength beneath her. Riding for her had so often been both a solution to a problem and an escape from situations she didn't want to face. On the back of a horse she couldn't let her attention wander. She had to focus on every footfall, be aware of every muscle in order to achieve that soaring sense of freedom that filled her very being. She wanted that freedom again.

Freedom from fear.

Freedom from witnessing her life instead of living it.

This sudden clarity in the muddied waters of her brain knocked her backwards into the nearest seat. Sink or swim her counselor had said. Just yesterday, when Samantha suggested the interview, she'd hesitated but seen no option but to agree. Was making that decision really all it took to turn her life around? Could she dare to hope for some understanding that would help her forgive herself?

Cameron, she had to call Cameron. Searching in her bag for her cell phone, she suddenly realized there was too much going on around her to make any sense of a telephone conversation. Reluctantly she left her phone where it was. She'd call him in the morning and arrange to see him so that she could explain everything before her story hit the news. If it even made a blip on that particular horizon anyway.

He'd treated her with care and respect. He'd been patient with her fears. He'd loved her into oblivion, whether he'd felt as much as she or not. For that at the very least she owed him an explanation.

Frustrated that it would have to wait, she tried instead to concentrate on the show, watching the performers through a haze of her own recollections. Memories that she had tried to block came tumbling back into her mind faster than she could process them, a kaleidoscope of color and confusion. Greybird, her first pony. The red and white pole of the first fence they ever jumped. Show jackets, hard hats. Dressage lessons. Her father instructing her in a voice like thunder to get her heels down.

She covered her ears and dropped her head, shaking it to drown out a lifetime of sights and sounds that turned in her mind like a carousel. How could there have been so much?

A procession of dogs, Labradors for her parents, mutts from an animal shelter for her. Making up feeds, filling haynets. The favorite titles on her bookshelf. School. Pay attention, Patricia. Her mother saddling Hawk, her first show jumper. And then Delacourt. Beautiful, black Delacourt prancing through her mind as easily as he had pranced into her life from the moment he was foaled. Speed, flight, fences.

Tony, no, not Tony. Not ready to face that betrayal all over again.

The thoughts came faster and faster, as dizzying as driving into a snowstorm, a whirlwind that left her breathless. Someone tapped her on the shoulder.

"Are you alright?" the woman behind her asked.

"Yes, thank you," Trisha stammered. "Just a bit light headed. I think I must be tired."

"Here, have this." The woman handed her a bottle of water. "Might be you're a bit dehydrated too. It's been a warm one today."

Trisha thanked her, gratefully took the bottle and drank her fill. When she looked up she couldn't quite believe that the show's finale had begun. If asked she would say it was spectacular, but to describe any of it in detail would be beyond her. She got to her feet, thanked the woman behind her again and headed for the exit. For now she wanted nothing more than to get home, have a shower, put on clean clothes and sleep.

Tomorrow she would talk to Cameron.

He would either understand, or not.

The crowd flowed in a never ending stream down the stairs and out of the doors. Tricia hitched the strap of her bag over her shoulder and prepared to skip down the final flight of steps, but a sudden prickle of awareness caused a hitch in her breath and made her stop.

She wouldn't have to call him. He was here, right behind her. Now beside her. She looked up into a pair of smoky-grey eyes that gleamed with humor.

"Didn't think I'd see you again," he said. He tipped his hat to her and swept past her, hand in hand with the blonde girl in pink cowboy boots.

Trisha stared at his retreating back in disbelief. For a moment she had the oddest sensation of shrinking, of collapsing into herself as if left with no substance. How could he do this to her? She stood immobile until she gathered her stunned senses and stumbled on with the rest of the crowd heading for the transit station.

While she waited for the train she recalled all the time she'd spent with Cameron, the moments when he'd made her feel wanted and loved and human again. Was all that a lie? It couldn't be, she didn't want it to be but had to face the truth of it. Gathering up what little dignity she had left, she braced her shoulders and stood upright as the train drew in to the station.

She didn't owe Cameron Carter anything.

She wouldn't speak to him or see him again.

Chapter Seventeen

"Are you quite comfortable, Trisha? Is there anything I can get you before we start?" Bryan Ross, Samantha's sympathetic journalist friend, placed a digital recorder on the desk.

Trisha eyed the recorder and swallowed. She had one similar to Bryan's, had used it over and over again and not once considered how her interviewees may have felt at some of the probing questions she'd asked.

A lifetime ago she had answered questions put to her by sporting journalists after successes at major three-day event venues. On more than one occasion she'd been interviewed in television studios but now her palms were clammy and her fingers trembled. With the interview about to begin she desperately wished she had not agreed to it, could be anywhere else but here in Samantha's office.

She shook her head. "No, thank you. I'm fine. I just want to get it over with."

"I understand." Bryan flashed an encouraging smile at her. "It's just you, me and Mike and you won't hear a peep out of him. He just runs the camera. So if you're ready?"

Trisha nodded. Bryan switched on the recorder.

"This is Bryan Ross with equestrian photojournalist Tricia Watts. Today is

Thursday, the time two o'clock pm. Interview starting at," Bryan looked at his watch, "two-oh-one pm."

Bryan had a notepad on his lap and a sheaf of papers in one hand. From what Trisha could see, it looked as if he had downloaded and printed a lot of information.

"I'm interested in the career you followed prior to your present occupation," he began, "so, in your own words, can you tell me about that?"

Trisha licked her lips. Seconds ticked by. At one time in her distant past she had been full of confidence, still could be when involved on an assignment, but her barely recovered ego still did not want to acknowledge what had been so excruciating for her.

Bryan leaned forward, the expression in his brown eyes kind and earnest. "I understand your apprehension. You had a frightening experience and reliving it must be painful, but your story might help others to find their feet again. Do you want a moment to regroup?"

An image of Brent Heywood's smiling face formed in her mind. No, she didn't need a moment. The time was right to put so many issues in their respective places. She shook her head.

"No thank you. But perhaps you could ask me a direct question? I think that would help me over the first hurdle."

Bryan grinned. "Great. You'll be fine."

And she was. Bryan asked a few questions which she thought about before answering, but then she became more relaxed and talked about her childhood and teenage years, the horses her mother raised and the riders her father trained.

"From everything you've told me so far," Bryan prompted, "you really were a rising star in the three-day event world."

"I wouldn't go that far, but because I had the benefit of such a talented horse we did have a chance at the title," Trisha agreed.

"Perhaps you could explain why it's such a popular sport in Europe?"

Trisha sat back. "It's a sport that grew from the methods used to train cavalry horses to show suppleness and obedience, strength and endurance and still have the ability to recover and have the stamina to compete in show jumping. It's like a triathlon for horses."

"But accidents happen?"

Trisha paused, knowing that question would be put to her, dreading having to answer. "Yes. We were about half way round a cross-country course. My horse Delacourt tripped before a fence but I brought his head up and we cleared it. He stumbled a little when we landed and I thought he might be going lame. I nearly pulled him up but then he galloped on so smoothly I carried on. He stumbled again as we approached a combination of a log and post-and-rails fence. I should have pulled him up there but I didn't. I pushed him and he gave a huge jump but when he cleared the log he kept going down and down. I can still see the ground rushing up at me. I, I …"

"Give yourself a breather here, Trisha." Bryan turned to his cameraman and made a cutting motion across his throat with his hand. "We'll take a few minutes for you to settle yourself before we start again. Can I get you a drink of water or a coffee?"

Trisha fisted her hands to stop them from trembling. Confession was supposed to be good for a person but she felt nauseous. Her legs felt heavy yet with no weight to them and she thanked the stars she was sitting down. She was not sure that she could have stood if she'd had to.

"Water, please," she said, her voice breaking.

Bryan left the room and came back with a glass of water for her and a bottle each for him and Mike.

"I can appreciate how difficult this must be for you," Bryan said. "Reliving such an experience can't be easy."

"No, it's not," Trisha said. She finished her water, blotted her lips with the napkin Ross had thoughtfully provided and nodded to him. "Thank you. I'm fine now. Shall we continue?"

Ross gave Mike a thumbs-up signal to start the camera again.

"What did the vets have to say about your horse?" Ross asked. "I guess there must have been an autopsy."

"Yes, of course." Trisha swallowed the hurt that still arose when she had to think of it. "Delacourt had passed all the vet checks, had shown no signs of any problem but he suffered a brain aneurism. My own vet thought it had likely happened when I felt him stumble the first time, but adrenalin and momentum kept him going."

"So you suffered serious injury yourself."

Trisha pressed her lips together then nodded. "I sustained a head injury and spent eight weeks in a coma, another two weeks in hospital after I came out of it and was in therapy after that."

"You mean physiotherapy?"

"That and," Trisha halted, choking on the admission she was about to make, "psychological counseling. After I'd more or less recovered physically I found that I'd lost my nerve. Any horseman will tell you to get back into the saddle after a fall. But it wasn't just any fall. My vet told me that even if I had pulled him up, Delacourt would probably still not have survived. But I don't know that for sure. My mistake killed a good, brave horse and I couldn't face it happening again. So I stopped riding and turned to photography."

Bryan reached across to her, put his hand on her knee and mouthed 'well done.' He gave her a moment before he went on to his next question.

"Had you always enjoyed photography?"

"Yes," she said. "I'd been given my first camera as a birthday present when I was fifteen and found that I had a knack for it. It's presented me with different opportunities and given me a good career."

"Including being invited to judge Purple Plain's cover model competition?"

Trisha nodded and dug deep to summon a smile. "One of my more fun assignments, I must say."

After a few more questions Bryan closed the interview and switched off the recorder. Trisha took a deep breath, thankful it was over but before she could get to her feet Bryan held up a hand to stop her.

"Trisha, before we close can I get a couple more shots of you?"

"Yes, if you have to. What do you want me to do?"

"Look straight into the camera." Trisha looked into that impersonal glass eye. "I want you to think of one thing that made you really sad."

Trisha flicked him a glance. Hadn't he been listening? The whole last two years of her life had been sad, but to pick one thing? She caught her lip, heard her father's voice again telling her how sorry he was that Delacourt, the one thing she loved more than anything else, was gone. No more slipping into his stable at night to whisper her concerns and fears into his willing ears. No more soft, silky neck to lay her head against and relax into his warmth.

"Good, Trisha, that's really good," Bryan murmured as he watched the emotions play across her face. "Now I want you to think of something that makes you very happy, just for us to finish on a good note."

"Happy?" Trisha stared at him in surprise. Happy. Did he know what he was asking?

"Yes," Bryan persisted. "However brief the moment, there must be something that grabbed your heart in its fist and warmed you through and through."

Trisha closed her eyes and thought of Cameron's smoky-grey eyes with their thick fringe of lashes, remembered the sensation of his long, strong fingers trailing over her skin. Remembered seeing him hand-in-hand with the blonde girl, remembered the sinking sensation in the pit of her stomach.

She'd allowed a handsome face and a kind manner to overturn her usual good sense. She had no one to blame but herself. Not a happy thought. But there had been moments, fleeting though they were, when everything had seemed so right.

Suddenly the casual photograph she'd taken of Cameron with the mare and foal came into her mind. She'd captured Sweetpea nudging his elbow and Rosie nuzzling his face. His expression had been one of pure and simple contentment. He'd been totally at peace with himself and his environment.

Her own life might be a bubbling mess, but at least she had pride in her work.

She turned to face the camera and smiled.

* * *

Brent idly flicked the pages of the magazine he'd picked up in the motel lobby. Being in no position to join the back-slapping, beer-swigging guys in the bars or the long-legged lovelies hovering at patio parties, he'd spent most of the week in his room in an effort to conserve his dwindling funds. To relieve his boredom he ventured out only during the evenings. He managed to lift a few wallets, but now that so many people recognized him he had to walk the tightrope of caution. Getting caught for petty theft at this stage would do him no good at all.

After Saturday it wouldn't matter, though he doubted the prize check would last long once he cashed it but at least he could party some. Whoever won the contest would sign their contract the same day and he could be in a photo shoot as early as the following Monday. How much were they paying? He should have read the contract terms more thoroughly. He couldn't remember any of the terms or the proposed rate and reached into his laptop bag for the publishing house's paperwork. He'd only skimmed over it when he first received it and now pulled out the sheaf of papers to read the details in full. It would be useful to know how soon after a shoot he could expect to be paid.

The television, his only form of company right now, played quietly in the background. He glanced up at the screen from time to time, paying no real attention to it until the daily round-up of news from the Stampede.

"Join us after the break," the announcer invited, "for an in-depth interview with Trisha Watts, the international photo-journalist who has the unenviable task of picking a winner for the Purple Plain Publishing house's cover model competition."

Brent frowned. What the hell was she up to? He reached for the remote and turned up the volume. The news anchor, a pretty brunette with a wide smile and not a hair out of place, introduced the interviewer and Trisha.

He listened in total disbelief as she answered the questions asked of her, slowly revealing every fact he'd threatened her with. She choked a little when she talked about how she'd lost her nerve after her accident and how she had wanted to keep that fact to herself. The news crew had even found a video of her competing on her black horse for Christ's sake.

Enraged, he leaped up from his chair, scattering papers everywhere.

The bitch, the stupid bitch. He raked his hands through his hair in sheer frustration and walked in circles, breathing hard.

First prize. Gone.

The agency contract. Gone.

The book cover award. Gone.

Everything he'd counted on disappeared in a haze of helpless fury. His hand curled into a fist. He plowed it again and again into the back of the chair in which he'd been sitting until he was breathless.

Think. Think.

What could he threaten her with now? The photographs he'd taken of Carter and his girlfriend would shatter her confidence all over again but that would barely give him any satisfaction at all at having his ambitions wrecked. No, it would have to be something more concrete than that, something that would hurt her more deeply, something that she could not walk away from, something that she would do anything to prevent.

What had she said?

My mistake killed a good, brave horse and I couldn't face it happening again.

He halted in mid-stride. That was it. She'd given him the answer he needed. Now all he had to do was track her down and face her with an ultimatum.

* * *

Despite Brent's best efforts he didn't catch up with her until Friday afternoon, and then only by constantly patrolling the photography display area in the exhibition hall. Once he caught sight of her, he made sure there were several people between them. He didn't want her spotting him and shaking him off before he had a chance to deal with her. His mouth pressed into a grim line as he watched her talk to people filling out and posting ballot forms.

He couldn't hear the conversation but whatever was said made her laugh.

The sound of it set him on edge and his jaw tightened. When he was done with her she'd regret having tried to better him.

After what seemed to him an interminable time, she moved away from the table holding the ballot boxes. Satisfied that she was alone, he trailed behind her out of the main doors and caught up with her as she headed towards the station exit.

"Done for the day, Patricia?" He deliberately made his voice as hard and cold as he could as he stepped up beside her and took her arm. "No, don't struggle. You and I are going to have a little talk."

He spun her around and pushed her down on a bench, then planted a booted foot beside her on the edge of the seat and rested his arm across his thigh. He'd succeeded in pinning her in place without actually touching her. He saw with satisfaction the alarm in her eyes as she shrank away from him. He crowded her so that she pressed back against the bench as far as she could then he leaned in so only she could hear him.

"I saw your interview," he hissed from between clenched teeth. "That was a bad move on your part, Patricia, really bad."

She licked her lips nervously. Good. He had her right where he wanted her and continued to glare at her.

"I told you I couldn't swing anything for you," she stammered. "The interview was the only way I could think of making that clear to you."

"Oh, you made that very clear. But I'm not finished with you yet." He straightened up very slightly, enough to not attract attention from passersby, not that anyone appeared to be interested in them but still, he couldn't be too careful. He smiled at her, as if they were having nothing more than a pleasant conversation. "You wouldn't want anything to happen to your boyfriend's horse, would you?"

He had the satisfaction of seeing the color leave her face and her eyes widen in disbelief.

"You wouldn't," she gasped. "You couldn't get anywhere near him, anyway."

"Are you sure about that?" His mouth twisted into a smile. "You don't know who I know, or how easy it would be for me to get back into the barns. It would be a shame if something happened to that horse's legs. There are any number of injuries, both big and small, that would put it out of action for months, if not years. Or, worst of all, bad enough for it to be euthanized. And it would be so easy."

He saw the fear in her face and removed his foot from the bench. He considered showing her the photographs on his phone of Carter and his girlfriend but thought better of it. Reminding her of Carter's cheating ways might back-fire on him if she decided she couldn't care less.

He stared down at her white face. She sat still as a stone and he knew how thoroughly he'd unnerved her. He tipped his hat to her and sauntered away, sure that he had her right where he needed her. She had no option now but to give in to his demands.

Victory would be so sweet.

Chapter Eighteen

Trisha watched Brent's retreating back, half expecting him to glance over his shoulder and smirk with satisfaction at her.

He couldn't really mean to harm the horse, he just couldn't. But was that a risk she dared take? Her hands trembled as she clutched the strap of her bag, rose from the bench and continued on her way to the station.

As furious as she was with Cameron for being a cheat and a liar, she couldn't bear the thought of another accident and another horse's life on her conscience. Nor, in spite of everything that had happened, did she want to jeopardize Cameron's chances of winning.

You're a fool, she told herself as the train sped into the downtown core. She'd allowed herself to be swept off her feet by a sexy cowboy who'd made her feel good about herself again. How fleeting a sensation was that. She would either have to ignore Heywood's threat and live with the consequences, or put aside her hurt and warn Cameron.

She chewed on her lip as she considered how she might do that. Every time he'd phoned her she had simply ignored his call. If she tried to phone him now, would he do the same to her? By the time she reached the condo she'd made a decision. However much she didn't want to, she had to see him and the only way she could do that was to drive out to Coyle Creek.

At her request to use the car, Samantha gave her the keys with no more than a sigh and a slightly raised eyebrow.

"I won't be long," Trisha told her and added a quick thank you.

On the previous occasions she'd been out to Cameron's place, he'd driven. On her own she found the drive tedious and wanted nothing more than to floor the accelerator to get there as quickly as she could. Cameron might already be back from the Stampede, but if not she would have to wait for him or simply leave a note on his door. Tapping her fingers impatiently on the steering wheel, she quelled the urge to put her foot down and send the car hurtling down the highway.

Her stomach churned with nerves by the time she turned in at the ranch gateway. She desperately hoped he wasn't there and her wish seemed to have been granted. As she crawled along the driveway there was no sign of the dogs or his truck. She'd just parked the car and stepped out of it when the door of the house opened. She couldn't turn back now.

He nursed a coffee mug in one hand, dropped into one of the chairs as casually as could be and propped his feet up on the veranda railing, something she'd never seen him do. She frowned. If this was how he wanted to play it, she would be as cool and uncaring too. She reached the steps and stopped, her feet suddenly unwilling to climb the shallow treads.

"Hey, babe," he said quietly. "What's up?"

"Babe?" She halted, unsure if his greeting was purposely callous or merely indifferent. "You've never called me babe."

"You don't like it?" His grey eyes regarded her coolly from beneath the brim of his hat.

Trisha stared at him, not sure that she even knew this man even though she'd shared his bed and his body. She shook her head. "No, I don't. You can call Barbie a babe, but not me."

"So what would you prefer?"

She preferred to not be there at all. She swallowed as she remembered the passionate moments they'd shared and her voice was husky when she answered, "I liked it when you called me sweetheart."

"All right, sweetheart it is." He paused and she hated the flat sound of his voice. "So what can I do for you?"

She swung up the rest of the steps and propped her back against the veranda post, hoping he wouldn't sense her agitation. Two could play at this game and if that was the way he wanted it, she would be as offhanded as he.

"It's not what you can do for me," she said as calmly as she could, "it's what I can do for you."

He shrugged one of his impressive shoulders and took a sip from his mug as if he couldn't care less. His sheer disinterest deflated her more than she could have imagined. Sapped of the little strength she'd arrived with she slumped against the post.

"It's Brent Heywood," she said.

"Brent who?"

"Oh, for heaven's sake." Stung by his apparent lack of perception, anger flared through her like a zap of electricity and she snapped to attention. "I told you. He's the guy who threatened to expose my real identity if I didn't declare him the winner of Purple Plain's cover model competition. That's the only reason I agreed to that television interview."

Another shrug. "Sorry, I didn't see it."

"I'd be surprised if you did," Trisha said bitterly, "but you might have heard about it if you'd been in any way interested."

"Okay, I'm interested. So what's up with this Heywood guy?"

"He's threatened me again." Trisha forced the words past the lump in her throat. "Only this time it's an indirect threat. He knows that we've been together, that you're likely to be in the steer wrestling finals and if I don't declare him the winner of Purple Plain's competition he's threatening to harm Anchorman."

In a sudden lunge he hauled himself out of the chair and slammed his mug down on the railing. The force of the blow cracked it in half. Coffee spilled from between the broken pieces, dripping over his fingers where he still gripped the handle. She'd wanted a reaction, any reaction, but she didn't know how to handle the white-hot fury she saw in his eyes and took a step back. This side of Cameron was a new and unwelcome revelation.

"When? How?" he barked.

She gulped in air to steady herself. "I don't know but you have to make sure Anchorman is watched, that he'll be safe. Whatever we had or didn't have," she nearly choked on the words and finished on a sob, "doesn't mean I'd willingly spoil your chances of winning your last Stampede by letting your horse get hurt."

Trisha ran down the steps and raced to the car before he could say anything else. She half expected to hear him pounding along in the dust behind her to ask for more information but, when she slid into the driver's seat, she saw him still on the veranda staring after her, his face a mask of anger.

She drove as if the devil were in her dust, zipping past cars as if they were standing still, changing lanes as fast as she could blink the tears from her eyes. What was the matter with these people? Why didn't they move? She dashed the back of her hand across her wet cheek and then glanced at her speedometer.

One hundred and thirty five kilometers an hour.

She couldn't believe the figures on the dial. She needed a speeding ticket like yesterday's news so slowed down and finished the trip back to town within the posted limits. When she pulled into Samantha's parking stall she cut the engine and collapsed her head on top of the steering wheel.

Damn Cameron Carter.

He only had to raise an eyebrow to send a surge of overwhelming wanting through her. Her head told her it was lust but a small part of her heart, the part that wanted to heal and be whole again, told her it was something else. Something precious and worth hanging on to.

But what about the other girl?

He had outright denied knowing her and she'd believed him. But those other occasions when he'd seemed to not know her and look right through her? What did that tell her? Was there something she'd missed?

Thinking about him made her heart pump so painfully she forgot to breathe. He'd hurt her in the worst possible way by not only cheating on her but flaunting that girl in her face. Whatever they had had together was of such short duration it didn't matter. Just as well she hadn't been more involved with him. She didn't owe him anything at all and would soon be gone.

She swung her legs out of the car and quickly stood up but her vision instantly blurred and her lungs constricted. Her knees almost gave way and she hung on to the top of the car door to support herself. Blowing out one breath she drew in another, held her side as if she'd been running and waited for her pulse to return to its regular, steady beat.

When she reached the apartment she was thankful to find it empty. Right now she didn't want to have to talk to anyone, just wanted to retreat into herself and hold all of her hurts in that familiar tight knot in her stomach.

Chilled to the bone she wandered to the window to warm herself in the rosy glow of the late evening sunlight. Below her the river swept past, the pathway along its shore line bustling with families out walking with their children, cyclists dodging past them, and lovers holding hands or with their arms around each other.

That sight made her miss Cameron and chiding herself for being foolish, she went to her room and pulled out her laptop. She checked her emails and then worked on her article, making a few revisions to what she had already written. She knew she would have to make more before she was completely finished.

She clicked onto her online calendar, relieved to see she only had one more official engagement to go, the final of Purple Plain's competition on Saturday afternoon. The Stampede finished on Sunday; her departure flight details were entered for Wednesday. She couldn't wait that long to leave.

Without any hesitation she logged onto her travel account and changed the date of her return flight.

Chapter Nineteen

Trisha drew back the heavy curtain and peered out at the audience.

"There are twice as many people here than for the opening night," she whispered.

Samantha took her turn at peering through the opening. "That's because Marguerite invited all their readers who'd helped with the draw count."

"She was so positive they'd get it wrapped up by noon." Trisha let the curtain drop and stepped off the stage. "But I still can't believe they did it. What an achievement."

"With time to spare," Samantha agreed. "Marguerite told me they were relaxing with coffee and donuts by eleven o'clock this morning."

Trisha flicked a glance to the back of the stage and grinned. "I think it's quite a novel idea to stack all the boxes of draw tickets the way they have done with the easels behind them. It looks a bit like they are all in a fort."

"Actually that was my idea." Samantha looked very pleased with herself. "It's in honor of Fort Calgary. I thought it rather went with the Stampede theme."

Marguerite, resplendent in turquoise and silver jewelry, a beaded and fringed deerskin jacket, black broomstick skirt and highly polished boots, approached and smiled broadly at them. "Everything's under control. I had a word here and there and Brent's been under surveillance. I don't think you have a thing to worry about, Trisha, but I do wish you'd agree to finish off the event by making the presentation to the winner."

Trisha shook her head. "That honor's all yours. I've done my bit but I am curious. Who scored the most draw tickets?"

A genuinely amused chuckle burst from Marguerite. "That's rich coming from the lady who said she had a week to make her decision for picking the winning photograph. You'll just have to wait."

With that she swept to centre stage and waited for the curtain to rise.

A murmur of voices and a shuffling of feet made Trisha look round. She saw six of the contestants being shepherded into place by a stage hand. She searched their faces and breathed a sigh of relief when she realized Brent Heywood was not amongst them and must be on the far side of the stage. She nodded to Jason Creevey, who grinned at her. The glint in his eye told her he didn't give a joe darn that she'd seen him practically in the buff. She gave a thumbs up sign to Greg Tooley and turned back to listen to the rest of Marguerite's presentation.

She crossed her fingers and sent up a silent prayer.

"And so we come to the part of the afternoon that everyone is waiting for."

Marguerite could hardly be heard above the racket from the ballroom. "But before I announce the number one model, I want to thank the Samantha Monroe Modeling Agency for producing this event. All the finalists will be offered a modeling contract with the Agency, but there is only one name on this piece of paper."

She produced a folded piece of paper and waved it above her head.

"We want it now," yelled someone from the middle of the crowd.

Marguerite smiled and leaned in to the microphone. "Before I reveal the winner, I would like you all to put your hands together for these fine gentlemen."

She called them one by one from alternate sides of the stage. As Jason Creevey passed Trisha he gave her a broad wink and she couldn't help but smile as he took his place in front of his photograph. Each professional studio shot was a replica of the tuxedo dressed contestant in front of it with not a naked body amongst them.

Marguerite waited until the applause died down. She fanned her face with the folded paper before leaning to the microphone again.

"All these gentlemen are winners in my book," another round of applause rippled through the room. "But," she unfolded the paper, took her time reading the name on it and paused again before looking along the line of hopeful faces behind her, "the winner from both the ballot and as selected by our judge is—Mr. Jason Creevey."

The noise in the room doubled as Jason stepped up beside Marguerite. He waved to the rowdy fans, handling his accolades with graceful good humor and none of the self-centered attitude she had sensed in some of the other entrants. With his kind of looks he could portray either a hero or a villain. Trisha smiled with satisfaction. At least she'd done something right.

"Was it because he was naked?" Samantha's eyes brightened with a hint of lasciviousness.

Trisha shook her head. "Nope. Believe it or not, it was simply the expression in his eyes. The photographer did a good job of capturing it and I'd love to know what she asked Jason to think of to draw it out of him in the first place. The others just didn't have that spark."

"She?" Samantha looked surprised.

"Oh, yes," Trisha chuckled. "I had to look at the photographers' credentials too. If they were complete amateurs I had to balance that with the overall criteria of what I was looking for. And don't you dare ever drop me into something like this again."

"Oh, get over yourself." Samantha snorted, but there was no censure in her voice. "Now, if you'll excuse me, I have to go and talk to all my lovely new men."

With a graceful turn Samantha slid away backstage. Trisha watched the contestants file off the stage but Jason stopped beside her and kissed her on the cheek.

"Couldn't resist me, could you?" he murmured in her ear.

She took no offense at his question, hearing in his voice the same self-mockery she'd seen in his eyes. This man just did not take himself seriously.

"Tell me something," she said, and laughed as he bowed over her hand and promised to tell her anything she wanted to hear. "What did your photographer ask you when she took your shower shot?"

Jason grinned. "She asked me to seduce her with my eyes. Guess it worked."

Trisha congratulated him and laughed as he walked away to join the group of guys gathering around Samantha. She frowned when she noticed that Brent Heywood was not amongst them. An uneasy tremor zigzagged down her back. She looked about her, concerned that despite Marguerite's promise she had everything under control. He might be loitering close by ready to accost her.

Before she could give Brent any more thought, Marguerite hurried up to her. Her cheeks were rosy with excitement and her blue eyes sparked.

"Come on," she said. "We're all going out to celebrate."

Trisha allowed herself to be caught up in the whirl of well being but a chilly uncertainty hovered at the edge of her enjoyment of the moment.

Just where was Brent Heywood?

*　*　*

"If you ask me," the girl with dark brown curls said as she took the stool beside him, "you were robbed."

Brent looked down at her with an expression of disdain on his face. "I didn't ask you."

The girl sighed. "Can't blame you for being out of sorts. Can I get you another beer?"

His grunt may have been a yes or a no but he slugged down the drink he already had. No point in missing out if some chick wanted to chat him up. "And a whiskey chaser."

"I'm Annie," the girl said by way of introduction after she'd ordered the drinks. "What do you plan to do now?"

Brent shrugged. He'd planned to party but there was fat chance of that now and his once bright future was alarmingly dim. "Move on now this is over, I suppose, but I haven't a clue where that might be."

Annie licked her lips suggestively. "Well, if you're not in too much of hurry, we could move on to my place. I could offer all sorts of consolation prizes."

Brent brightened a little at that. Free booze here and a bed for the night with her didn't sound like a bad deal at all. In anticipation of improving his accommodation, at least for the rest of the weekend, he'd already checked out of his motel. He had no intention of checking back in. He loosened up a little with the next round of drinks, some more with the round after that and was quite relaxed when Annie smiled invitingly at him and pressed a kiss on his cheek.

"Just tell me when you're ready to go," she told him.

"How about right now?" He stumbled slightly as he stood up. Hell, he hadn't drunk that much had he?

She took his arm and led him out into the car park where she helped him into her car. She smiled as he fumbled with the safety belt, finally took pity on him and fastened it for him.

"Where're we goin'?" Brent mumbled as he slumped back in his seat.

"I told you. My place. It's in Mission."

"Nice," Brent murmured.

Annie didn't think he knew where Mission was located, but it didn't matter. She drove around her block a few times while Brent snored lightly beside her. When she pulled into the curb outside of her house her room-mate, Tova, came out to meet her.

"How is he?" she asked.

"Sleeping like a baby," Annie replied. For the first time since she'd been asked to help, she frowned with sudden concern. "He won't be hurt, will he?"

"No," Tova assured her. "We've arranged an overnight trip for him just to get him out of the way for the rodeo finals tomorrow but we have to hurry. Do you want me to drive?"

Before they could swap seats Brent opened his eyes and struggled upright. He stared uncomprehendingly at the blonde girl standing beside the car.

"Are you an angel?" he croaked.

She reached into the car and stroked his cheek. "I am tonight, cowboy."

"Thas' all right then." His eyes fell closed with much less effort than it had taken to open them. As his head dropped down towards his shoulder he snored again. This time the snore was followed by the soft flutter of air as it escaped from between his slack lips.

"Whew," Annie breathed. "I thought he was going to wake up."

"Not for a long time," Tova told her. "Come on, get in the back and let me drive. It'll be easier than giving you directions."

Annie slipped into the back seat and had barely buckled up before they were on the move again. Brent's head rocked against the seat as they turned corners, settled again as they waited for lights to change and didn't move again as they continued their trip. Annie wasn't sure where they were going, but at last Tova turned into the parking lot of a big truck stop. She slowed to a crawl, looking left and right until she spotted a horse trailer. She stopped beside it and a large figure in plaid shirt and jeans got out of the truck.

"That's my boyfriend, Mack," Tova said with a chuckle, having caught sight of Annie's startled expression in the rearview mirror.

"Hey, babe, any problems?" Mack asked as he opened the door for her.

"Nope. It all worked like a charm." Tova got out of the car, slipped her arms around Mack's waist and hugged him. "Oh, and by the way, did you know I'm an angel?"

Annie didn't hear the muffled response as Mack reached into the car and hauled Brent's inert body out.

"Where are you taking him?" she asked.

Mack flashed a quick grin. "I'm not taking him anywhere. But my friend Wade Polanski here is. He didn't score enough points in the wagon racing this week to make it worth his while staying to the end of Stampede, so he's heading on up to Grande Prairie and the Peace country to see what damage he can do there."

"Whoa, bud," Wade objected as he opened the trailer door. "Less of that damage talk. Here, tumble that fella inta' this stall beside my gear."

Between them the two men propped Brent's slumbering body into an empty stall between a stack of harness and a pile of blankets while the already loaded horses munched on hay, apparently unperturbed at their strange travelling companion.

Wade closed and secured the door while Mack dusted off his jeans.

"What'd he do anyway?" Wade asked as they shook hands.

"He threatened to put my brother's horse out of action."

"Hell," Wade grunted. "That ain't right. Cameron's got a chance tomorrow then?"

Mack grinned broadly. "Best he's ever had."

Wade tipped his hat to the girls and got back into his truck. He turned the engine, let it run for a few seconds then hauled out of the lot with a final wave of his hand to Mack.

"Okay, ladies," Mack said as his friend rolled away down the road, "what would you like to do for the rest of this evening?"

"Go to the Ranchman's," said Tova, slipping her arm through his. "How 'bout you, Annie?"

"Sorry to be a bore, guys." Annie covered a yawn with the back of her hand." If it's all the same to you, I'm going home. All this subterfuge stuff has worn me out. By the way, what exactly was it I dropped in Brent's drink?"

Tova chuckled. "Just a dose of benzo. He'll sleep like a baby tonight and probably have a bit of a hangover tomorrow, but Mack gave Wade some money to give to him so he won't be destitute. We're probably kinder to him than he deserves, but at least he can't do any harm if he's out of the way. Want to come to the rodeo finals with us tomorrow?"

"I'd love to but I'm afraid I can't," Annie said as she got into her car. Mack folded himself in beside her and Tova scrambled into the back. "I'm on duty tomorrow and have to be at the airport for three o'clock. After all this, I hope your brother wins Mack."

Mack acknowledged her good wishes with a brief nod but a soft expression settled on his mouth. He'd not been around much in the last few years but, regardless of the issues that had driven them apart, he wanted the best for his brother too.

"So do I Annie," he said. "So do I."

Chapter Twenty

"You intend leaving any hair on that poor critter's hide?"

Cameron took one more vigorous sweep over Anchorman's already spotless hindquarters. He threw the brush he used in a bucket with the rest of the grooming tools before he looked up.

His hazer, Larry McKinley, leaned easily against the end of the stall.

"Guess I'm just a tad leery about starting the big one this afternoon." To Cameron it was a better reason than admitting he couldn't get Trisha Watts out of his mind. He'd missed talking with her, teasing her, making love with her.

Heck, he'd even slept on the couch a couple of nights because he didn't want to get into bed and her not be in it with him. What they had together went so far beyond sex and he'd thought she felt it too. Not that he'd had a chance to ask her as she hadn't taken any of his calls or answered the voicemail or text messages he'd sent her. Missing her and worrying about her rankled worse than a burr under his saddle and at the end of the afternoon, win or lose, his first order of business would be to track her down. He reached into the bucket and pulled out a mane comb, aware all the time of Larry's steady gaze on his back.

"Uh-huh." Larry drawled, not sounding at all convinced. "Rumor has it this is your last Stampede."

"For once, rumor is right." Cameron combed out Anchorman's mane but gave up when the horse shifted away from him. He sent the comb the same way as the brush.

"If that's the case, why isn't Mack here?"

"Aww, come on, Larry." Disgust filled Cameron's voice. "You know why he's not here."

"Can't blame him for wanting to follow his own path and not yours." Larry shifted his weight against the side of the stall as Cameron pushed past him.

"Yeah, whatever." Cameron walked out into the aisle with Larry following him. He stepped around bales of hay and a wagon full of fresh, sweet smelling wood shavings. He strode outside the barn with Larry right beside him.

"Wouldn't hurt my feelings none if you wanted your brother in at the end," Larry continued.

"Nope." Cameron shook his head emphatically. "You and me have got this gig down to a fine art. We've worked together how long now?"

"Since your Ma and Pa died. So ten years, give or take."

"There you go then. Too long to risk changing it up at the last moment. See you later."

Larry's question churned in Cameron's stomach as he walked away. It was true he and Mackenzie had been a good team, the operative word there being 'had'. When their parents died they discovered that their ranch carried not only a second, but a third mortgage and for the first time they fully realized how their rodeo careers had been financed. He'd been willing to do whatever it took to keep the ranch but not his brother.

He could still taste the bitter disappointment of Mackenzie's refusal to pitch in and help save the place they'd called home all their lives. And then Mack put ranching and rodeoing behind him and joined the military. Going from leaning on each other for support, company, rivalry and anything else they could cook up as brothers, to standing alone took some getting used to.

Cameron's mouth settled into a tight line. Larry said Mack couldn't be blamed for going his own way but Cameron did blame him. He hadn't even stuck around long enough to help out after the funeral and he lived his brother's defection every single day. It irked him worse than a pebble in his boot. He flipped his hat off and raked his fingers through his hair, then settled the Stetson on his head again.

It didn't do to think about Mackenzie and what might have been. Today was too big a day to let anything cloud his judgment.

He walked some more, stretching out his back and legs, making sure he had no knots of tension ready to kink up his muscles at the wrong moment. He rolled his shoulders a couple of times and headed back to Anchorman's stall and started tacking him up.

A hand clapped him on his shoulder and he looked up from cinching the saddle into an older man's eyes. Tommy Conrad, a neighbor, with two daughters who both barrel raced.

"Your Ma and Pa would be right proud of you about now, I reckon."

"Thanks, Mr. Conrad." The old courtesy, insisted on by his mother in his formative years, still came easier to his lips than a casual 'Tommy'. The weight of the man's hand, a hand as big and as warm as his father's had been, comforted him as much as the words did.

He tested the cinch, tightened it again then swung into the saddle. Sensing his rider's tension, Anchorman snorted and danced sideways. Cameron laid a hand on the horse's neck, mentally calming himself. It wouldn't do any good at all to let his nerves get the better of either of them.

As he rode into the outfield he looked around for Larry, and frowned. There was no sign of him, or the rangy roan mare he always rode. Looking up and down the line of men lounging against the fence, the horses standing ready to compete, the tail end of one horse caught his eye and he almost choked.

He'd know that scrub-tailed paint gelding anywhere. And if it was here, that must mean ...

A man stepped into the arena and took the paint's reins, then mounted and rode towards him.

"That look could curdle milk, bro," Mackenzie grinned at his brother's shocked expression. "Couldn't resist partnering with you for your last big one."

"How in hell did you know about that?" Cameron growled. His jaw tightened as he bit back everything he'd like to say, knowing that if he started it would be difficult to stop until he'd blown every hurt at his brother out of his system.

"Ever heard of texting?" Mackenzie neck-reined his paint to ride along side his brother. "Larry kept me in the loop. Said you'd be too mule-headed to let me know yourself."

Before Cameron could loosen his tongue and shoot off an angry retort, the announcer introduced them as the Carter brothers, previous partners now re-uniting in a grand slam effort to win the big one. Still stunned at the turn of events, Cameron rode Anchorman into the starting box. He turned the horse around and backed him into the corner, catching Mackenzie's eye as he did so.

Mackenzie grinned at him, that slow, almost sardonic lift of his mouth so familiar it slammed into Cameron's gut. Hell, he'd missed

Mack like crazy, but he was here now, when it mattered most. He watched Mack line his paint up on the other side of the starting chute, a move he'd seen a thousand times but one that meant more to him today than at any other. Cameron grinned back at his brother, knowing with a deep-seated certainty that everything was going to settle into its rightful place in the world.

He glanced up at the clear blue sky, thankful for the perfect weather conditions. Anchorman could run in the mud if he had to, but the ground today would be ideal for him. The barrage of sound from the crowds in the grandstands almost deafened him. A brief image of his parents and how proud they would have been of him skimmed through his mind.

But then he looked at his steer being loaded into the chute, watched the starter fix the breakaway rope barrier and everything around him faded into oblivion.

His vision narrowed as he focused on the steer's brindle hide.

Sounds faded away by degrees until he could not even hear the blood pulsing through his head.

Anchorman quivered like a coiled spring beneath him, every muscle and tendon primed to shoot forward at the first signal. He barely sensed the horse's anticipation.

Everything he was, everything he had ever been, condensed into this one moment. He narrowed his gaze even more, pinning it on his steer until he saw nothing else. He nodded his head at the starter.

In an instant his world changed.

The steer charged from the chute, triggering the barrier.

Anchorman launched himself from the box, springing off his hocks in one powerful thrust.

One stride.

They were in the arena in a blur of motion.

Two strides.

Anchorman came alongside the steer.

Three strides.

Cameron leaned down from the saddle and caught the steer's left horn in a rock-hard overhand grip. He threw his right arm around the opposite horn and dropped in the hole between his horse and the steer, right where he needed to be, landing at the perfect angle to optimize his weight.

Anchorman galloped on, leaving his rider to plant his heels in the dirt. Cameron shifted his left hand from the steer's horn to its nose, tightened his grip and twisted as hard as he could.

They both dropped in the dirt.

Cameron got to his feet and took one quick look back at the barrier.

Good, they hadn't broken it.

He looked up at the clock and his jaw dropped.

Three seconds even.

The cheering and applause rocking the grandstand gradually filtered into his ears, and the wall of sound echoing around the infield totally engulfed him. A slow grin formed on his face. He grabbed the brim of his hat and threw it into the air. It soared high above him, swirling on an air current before falling to the ground.

He watched Mackenzie retrieve it, reaching down from the saddle to scoop it up in one smooth move. Anchorman trotted up and Mackenzie grabbed his reins and headed towards his brother.

"Good one, bro," he yelled. "You did it."

Cameron swung into the saddle and looked up at the grandstand. He hoped Trisha might be up there in the crowd. She'd been the first person he'd told of his decision to quit rodeoing after this Stampede. He would have liked it if she'd seen his last performance.

Mack caught his attention and pointed at a TV camera. They both faced it and waved at the cheering crowd before riding out of the arena.

* * *

"Have I been drinking today?" Samantha suddenly asked.

Trisha looked up from the souvenir brochure she'd been thumbing through for information on the next competitor. She'd tried to remain calm and disinterested as Cameron had backed Anchorman into the starting box, but her pulse still raced with the excitement of his astounding performance. She didn't see how he could be beaten. "I don't think so. Why?"

"There's two of them."

"Two of who?"

"Cameron, you ninny. Who'd you think I meant? Look."

Trisha looked up at the jumbotron screens fixed either end of the arena. They displayed images of two men, each wearing black hats, pink shirts and jeans. They rode side by side while they waved at the camera and the crowds, and then trotted out of the arena to be swallowed up by the cowboys at the entry gate.

Her mouth dropped open as her brain processed what her eyes saw. Her heart lurched and her mouth dried. She licked her lips and swallowed hard, still trying to make sense of what she'd seen. It couldn't be true.

"Twins," Samantha chortled, "identical twins."

"He said he had a younger brother," Trisha stuttered, her mind still trying to cope with the shock of the images she had just seen.

"Well one of them had to be born first." Samantha grinned broadly at her. "Obviously it was Cameron."

"He said his hazer was a guy called Larry," Trisha remembered, "but his brother is Mackenzie. Which means ..."

"Which means what?" Samantha prompted her.

"Mackenzie came back to help him win his last Stampede." Trisha's blood ran cold as another thought wormed its way into her mind. She shot out of her seat. "Oh. My. God."

Samantha, still wearing an expression of amusement, looked up at her.

"What?"

"I've got to go," Trisha muttered.

She grabbed her bag, swinging it over her shoulder so hurriedly that she almost hit the person sitting in the row behind her. She uttered an apology and pushed past Samantha who hurriedly gathered up her own belongings as she yelled at Trisha to wait.

Trisha didn't hear her as she ran down the steps to the closest exit, brushing people aside in her hurry to escape.

What a fool I've been.

Her heart pounded as she thought of the times she'd been with Cameron. Or had it been Mackenzie?

Which brother had she gone riding with? Which brother had teased her and eased the aftermath of her nightmares? And most of all, the realization of it almost shredded her heart, which brother had she fallen in love with?

Samantha caught up with her outside the grandstand and hauled her to a stop. "Why are you running away?"

"There's nothing for me here," Trisha stuttered. "Those idiots have been batting me between the two of them since the day I arrived."

"You don't know that for sure," Samantha argued.

"No? I've heard about twins dating each other's partners just for the hell of it or to help each other out." Trisha wrenched her wallet out of her bag and dug for change for her train ticket but dropped the coins.

She threw her hands wide in exasperation but Samantha had already saved her the trouble of retrieving them by producing two train tickets. She waved them under Trisha's nose.

"You need to calm down and look at this logically," she advised as they headed to the station.

"Logic?" Trisha was beyond herself. "Where's the logic in any of this, I'd like to know?"

By the time the train pulled into the platform Trisha had sunk into silence and Samantha gave up trying to get through to her. When they reached the condo Trisha went straight to her room where she cleared her belongings from the closet and bathroom and packed her bags. She ignored Samantha's pleadings for her to stay.

What was there to stay for? It didn't matter how much she thought she loved Cameron. That he could fool her by swapping roles with his twin brother told her everything she needed to know and that had nothing to do with love.

Samantha drove her to the airport, still insisting that Trisha should stay and at least give Cameron the benefit of the doubt.

"I wouldn't know what to say to him and I don't know if I could believe him," Trisha admitted. "Fool me once, shame on you. Fool me twice, shame on me. I think I've been fooled enough, thank you."

Trisha insisted that Samantha just drop her off at the terminal and not wait with her until her flight departed. She just wanted to be on her own, to sink into her own thoughts and try and sort them out.

"I should say thanks for everything," she said as they loaded a baggage cart, "even bullying me into that interview, but right now I can't even think straight."

"What do you want me to do if Cameron contacts me?" Samantha asked, determined not to let Trisha go without trying again to make her reconsider.

"You don't know me," Trisha said wearily. "You don't know where I live, you don't have any contact numbers for me, for all you know I don't even exist."

"You don't mean that," Samantha said. "You'll feel differently in a few days."

Trisha hugged her again. "Maybe."

She turned then and with a straight back and dry eyes entered the concourse. For thirteen days she hadn't known from one day to the next what she would have to deal with, whether it was how she felt about Cameron or what she feared most from Brent Heywood. She'd survived Samantha's plans and finally come face-to-face with the nightmare of her accident.

All she wanted now was to go home.

Chapter Twenty One

"So for how much longer are you going to sulk?"

Cameron shot his brother a warning glare but Mackenzie, lounging comfortably against the wall, ignored him.

"She made her choice," Cameron muttered as he forked fresh wood shavings across the stable floor.

"I doubt it was a good one for either of you."

Cameron's jaw tightened. It didn't help that he'd had to tell Mack everything about Trisha in order to explain his foul mood after winning the most prestigious event of his career. He hadn't been able to find her on that last day of Stampede or, as yet, had the time to connect with Samantha Monroe to get an address or telephone number from her. There'd been far too much to do in preparation for his upcoming training clinic. At least, that was his rationalization to cover the fear that Trisha really didn't want to see him or hear from him again. That fear crept into his consciousness too many times during the day and haunted his sleep at night.

"What would you know about making good choices?" Cameron growled.

"A helluva lot more than you it seems."

"Name one." Cameron whirled around to stare his brother down.

"Leaving you to stew after Ma and Pa died," Mack said quietly.

Cameron's hands curled into fists and bile rose in his throat as his brother so blatantly voiced the core of the problem between them.

"Go on," Mack goaded. "Hit me if you think you'll feel better."

They hadn't had a fist fight since their father had caught them slugging it out behind the barn when they were thirteen. Instead of stopping them, he'd hauled them back to the house and insisted they carry on the fight in front of their mother. Under her unwavering glare they had thrown a few more punches at each other before letting their hands drop to their sides, the argument that set them off forgotten.

With supreme effort Cameron uncurled his fists and flexed his fingers, knowing that Mackenzie remembered that day too. He swallowed hard. "We both know that won't solve anything but, since you brought it up, why did you leave?"

Mack didn't give an immediate answer but went to the entrance of the barn and looked outside. "Would you have all of this if we'd stayed at the home place?"

"That's not the point," Cameron began as he joined his brother in the doorway.

"That's exactly the point." Mack huffed out a breath of frustration. "We were too young to be saddled with a load of debt that we didn't make. Don't get me wrong, I loved Ma and Pa, but do you remember what a tough bastard he could be if we didn't get placed high enough for his liking when we competed?"

"He wanted the best for us." Cameron's jaw tightened stubbornly in defense of his father.

"No, that wasn't it at all." Mack shook his head. "He wanted us to be the best for him, because he never made it. If he hadn't have busted his leg so bad just after we were born, how much do you think we'd have seen of him? He'd never have settled down or we'd have been hauled all over hell's half acre to suit him. How fair would that have been on Ma, or us for that matter?"

"She'd have gone anywhere with Pa," Cameron insisted. "She loved him."

"Sure she did," Mack agreed. "But that didn't mean she liked him a lot of the time."

Cameron frowned, suddenly unsettled that Mack might have had some insights into their parents that he'd missed. "What's that supposed to mean?"

Mack hooked his thumbs into his belt loops and looked miserable. "I didn't come here to hash up old hurts, but do you remember when Pa bought you that sorrel gelding?"

"Yeah, sure I do. We were just about to turn sixteen. What of it?"

"Ma was furious with him. That was your birthday present, not mine. In fact," Mack drew in a breath, "think about all the times you got something and I didn't."

"That's ridiculous." Cameron glared at his brother, but Mack had hit a nerve as surely as hitting a nail squarely on the head. "Anything Pa bought was for us to share."

Mack shook his head. "No, bro. It was all to help make you the big rodeo name he never was. We rubbed along because we steer wrestled which took the two of us. If you'd have wanted to ride broncs like Pa, and I'd been keen on the bulls, how would he have coped with coaching and providing for the two of us? Pa thought you had more potential than I did which was why he spent more time with you. Ma knew it and didn't like that about him. I heard them arguing over us more than once."

"And you never thought to tell me?" Hurt, laced with a measure of guilt, curled through Cameron's stomach.

"You wouldn't have believed me," Mack said and Cameron knew he was right. "You would have believed me even less if I'd tried to explain all that to you after the funeral. We were both hurting too much but for different reasons. But look what it did for us. You've got this place, I've got my house in town and a few other things here and there and neither of us have any debt. What we do have, we both own outright and the bank can't take it away from us. So do I know about making good choices?" The look in Mack's eyes dared Cameron to disagree with him. "Yeah, bro. I think I do."

For a moment neither of them spoke. Cameron tipped his hat forward and rubbed the back of his neck. He couldn't deny the truth of what Mack said. He'd been blind to it when they'd been boys, but during the time he'd dealt with the ranch dispersal, the accountant, taxman and the bank, he'd cursed his father more than once.

It hurt more than he could have imagined as the horses were sold off, one by one or a bunch of them, mostly to surrounding ranches. Same with the small herd of cattle they ran. Auction day had seen off the house contents and the heavy ranch equipment. Mack had kept nothing, while he'd salvaged his favorite saddle and a few mementos of their parents. When all the debts had been cleared and the taxes paid, they'd been lucky enough to have a small inheritance to share.

"Guess I have to agree with you," Cameron conceded. "And thanks for turning up for my final go-round. That was another good choice."

Mack chuckled. "You're welcome, but speaking of good choices, I made another one. Want to hear it?"

"Hit me."

"I've chosen you to be my best man."

Cameron felt his jaw drop and he stared in disbelief at his brother.

"I know." Mack threw out his hands in an expression of helplessness and reddened under Cameron's withering stare. "Last thing I thought would happen too, but our paths kept crossing and before I knew it I didn't want to be without her. Lucky for me she feels the same way. What do you say?"

Cameron didn't immediately have anything to say as he tried to unscramble his brains to accommodate the concept of his younger brother getting married. Along with that fact he heard again Trisha's accusations, asking him where he'd been and with whom and something in his mind clicked.

"Your bride-to-be wouldn't happen to have long blonde hair and wear pink boots, would she?"

"Wh-o-oa." Mack backed away from him and crossed his forefingers in the familiar sign of protection from evil. "Twins are supposed to be psychic but that's scary accurate, dude."

Suddenly suspicious, Cameron peered at his brother through narrowed eyes. "When exactly did you get into town?"

"Tuesday before Stampede started," Mack threw out casually.

"So where did you stay?" The suspicion in Cameron's mind grew stronger.

"Tova shares a house in Mission. Made more sense to go there than have her haul her stuff to my place. Why?"

Cameron slowly shook his head. "Un-freaking-believable."

Now Trisha's comments and the times she'd seemed mad at him made sense. She hadn't seen him, she'd seen Mackenzie and what was worse, he knew it.

"Before you explode," Mackenzie said, putting a hand on Cameron's chest and holding him at arm's length, "just let me say this in my own defense. Hiding in plain sight seemed to make the most sense. I've been gone long enough that most folks would almost forget you had a brother. I didn't want to see you until your final event because I didn't want any arguments about hazing for you. But Tova insisted I talk to you, so I came out to the ranch to see you."

"When?"

"Friday evening, but you weren't home so I waited a bit and then Trisha turned up. I'd seen her on the plane when I flew in, and then on the grounds, but didn't know until she pulled into the yard that you two were an item. Man, she had some ruffled feathers about some dude called Brent something or other."

"Heywood," Cameron muttered between clenched teeth.

"Yep, that was the name." Mack nodded his head in recognition. "Didn't understand half of what she was on about but as far as I could tell, if she didn't fix it for him to win some competition, he threatened to hurt Anchorman. That really upset her for some reason."

"You'd have to know her to understand that." Cameron scrubbed his hand over his face. "You're only just telling me this now?"

"I took care of it so I didn't see a reason to." Mack slid his hands into his pockets and shrugged.

"Took care of it how?" Cameron knew how his brother tended to take care of things. He squinted down the driveway to make sure there were no police cars driving up it to take Mack away.

"Being in the military had its uses. I learnt a thing or two about surveillance and still have friends in town to call on for back up. Both you and your horse had eyes on you since about, oh, seven-ten on Friday evening, Larry being in charge of the horse watch." A wicked chuckle bubbled out of Mack's throat. "And Brent Heywood got a one way ticket up north with Wade Polanski."

"Sheee-it." Cameron grabbed his hat off his head and slapped it across his thigh. "Guess you had my back in more ways than one so now I owe you all over again."

"And here's something else you owe me for." Mack drew a piece of paper out of his jeans pocket and handed it over.

Cameron unfolded it and looked blank until he realized what he was reading. "Trisha's home address? Where'd you get this?"

"Tackled the dragon lady in her den while you were dragging your heels." Mack rolled his eyes. "I must really love you, bro, because that one really is a piece of work. So when are you going to see your lady?"

"I can't leave now until after the clinic."

"Bullshit you can't," Mack roared in exasperation at his brother. "I'll teach the goddam clinic for you."

"You couldn't teach a frog to croak."

Instantly they were face to face and toe to toe with fists raised, glaring at each other in fury. Long seconds ticked by, each waiting for the other to land the first blow. Then Mack began to chuckle. Cameron dropped his fists and joined him. In moments they were both consumed with laughter, great gusts of it bellowing out from deep in their chests.

"Guess we're not thirteen anymore," Cameron wheezed as he caught his breath and his brother at the same time.

"Either that or we're the biggest damn thirteen-year olds that every walked the planet," Mack gasped, hugging his brother back. He wiped tears of relief laden laughter from his eyes. "Whew, that took me back."

Cameron slapped his brother's back. "Didn't it just? But I guess we both learned our lesson."

"Yeah, there are some things we have to thank Pa for." Mack straightened his Stetson. "Now big bro, tell me about this clinic of yours. How many people are coming? Is it basic horsemanship? Any problem horses to sort out? What do I need to know?"

With so many questions being fired at him Cameron almost forgot the paper Mack had handed him. When he looked at it again he reached for his phone, but hesitated. Trisha hadn't answered any of his calls while she'd been here so why think she'd answer him now?

He thought of the check he'd won at the Stampede, the quarter horse stud he'd purchased and arranged transport for over the phone. He looked with quiet pride at the home he'd built and with even more pride at his brother who had, when it mattered, been there for him. He had everything he wanted, but he didn't have the one thing he needed. Trisha.

He reached for the phone again and called the airline.

Chapter Twenty Two

Relieved to be in her own room and in her own bed again, after four days Trisha still could not sleep. Her body hadn't yet caught up with the time changes between Calgary and her English home, but more than that she knew Samantha had been right. She'd run away without facing up to whichever of the twins was Cameron. Added to that, Samantha had sent her a one word text.

Coward.

At first furious with her, Trisha finally admitted it when they spoke on the phone two days after she'd arrived home. Samantha had a lot to say and later that day Trisha had taken another call, a call that had given her much to think about.

Giving up on any thoughts of sleep now, she rolled out of bed and went to stand by her open window. She loved her hilltop home and never tired of the view out over the stable yard and riding arenas to the beech woods beyond. At this early hour a veil of light mist hung in the valley below her. It would soon burn off once the sun rose. Somewhere a cock crowed and she heard the rattle of buckets as the grooms started work in the yard.

Suddenly needing the activity she pulled on riding pants and a light sweatshirt, ran a brush through her hair and pulled it into a pony-tail. She ran down the stairs, out the back door and made her way to the feed room where her mother, always an early riser, handed her two pails.

"Seeing as you're up and about," she said with a smile, "would you take these to my boys?"

Trisha nodded and took the feed to the stallions, Croft Court and Winter Magic. Then she made her way around the rest of the horses, stroking noses and patting necks. It still amazed her how thirteen days in Calgary had made her realize how much she missed this routine. She stopped to lean on the paddock fence and watched several mares and foals grazing there. A dark bay foal came to inspect her, nudging her elbow which reminded her of the photo she had taken of Rosie and Sweetpea with Cameron.

She sighed and pressed her thumb between her eyebrows to relieve the tension that thinking of him produced. She owed him an apology and hadn't yet decided how best to do that. She didn't think he'd take her call if she phoned him. She might give him the wrong impression if she went back and delivered it in person. Yet she knew, for peace of mind and to ease her heart, she had to do something and soon.

Before she could come to any conclusions, her father strolled out to join her. He threw an arm around her shoulders.

"So Patti?"
"So Dad?"

He chuckled. "I've been watching the wheels spin round in your head and you're getting nowhere. At one time riding a horse helped you solve your problems."

"That was a long time ago."

"Why not give it a go now?" Her father dropped a kiss on her cheek. She tucked her hand in the crook of his arm and rested her head on his shoulder.

"You obviously have a horse in mind. Which one is it?"

Before her father could tell her, her mother hollered at her from the house.

"Patti, phone. It's that guy from Calgary. Come quick."

* * *

Cameron wasn't sure what he'd expected his first sight of England to be, but so much greenery wasn't it.

He peered out of the cabin window at hedgerows and trees that separated one field from another. Urban sprawl encroached into the countryside making the whole look like a patchwork quilt. A network of narrow roads crowded with ribbons of traffic tied this small country together and in no time at all he became part of that parcel.

Cab drivers at the airport had looked at the address he'd showed them on his phone's contact list and shook their heads. It was either unknown to them or too far for them to go. Then he found a cab willing to take him, at a price.

"'Course I take Visa," the driver assured him. "Just 'ave to let my dispatcher know where I'm off to. Doncha worry, Sunshine, I'll get ya there."

Once his driver had radioed the dispatcher with his destination, Cameron settled himself in the soft leather seat and stretched his legs. Not used to being driven and being on the other side of the road at that, all took its toll on him. He wanted to close his eyes and sleep, but determined to give a visitor to his country the benefit of his knowledge, the driver kept up a running commentary advising him to look at this or watch out for that.

The look of the countryside through which they passed changed. At first only a subtle shift, it then became more definite with open green spaces dotted with farms and cottages and much more tree cover than he'd expected. They skirted a small town, the houses stone-built and huddled together, dominated by a square church tower.

"This is Cirencester," his ever watchful guide announced. "Back in the day when the Romans settled here it was called Corinium Dobunnorum."

"You seem to know a lot," Cameron commented.

"Used to drive buses," the driver explained. "Been a few years since I last run this route, but

I 'aven't forgotten my stops." He checked his GPS. "Not long now, mate."

Cameron rubbed a hand along his jaw, feeling the scrub of overnight stubble. He wished now he'd at least stopped for a shave. His stomach knotted and all the thoughts he'd been trying to keep out of his head crowded back in. He desperately hoped Trisha would be at home. If she was already off on another assignment, his trip would have been wasted.

"We're here, guv," the driver announced. "Somerville Court."

Pulling himself out of his dark thoughts, Cameron's eyes widened at the sight of the tall, wrought iron gates through which they passed, the graveled forecourt beyond it and the graceful outline of the house overlooking it.

"Is this a mansion?" he asked, trying to take in the sweeping elegance of it.

"Close enough." The driver pulled up beneath a covered entrance way and Cameron unfolded himself from the back seat.

The supreme confidence that bolstered him while he waited for his steer to break out of the chute at the Stampede now fled, leaving him disoriented and jittery. Having arrived on Trisha's doorstep he felt all kinds of a fool. He turned to the cabby.

"I'm not sure how long I'm going to be," he said hesitantly. "Could you wait up somewhere?"

"Passed a pub a bit back, call me when you're ready." Cameron took the business card the driver handed him, and in return offered a couple of folded bills. The driver took them, looked at them and handed one back. "Thanks, guv, but I'm not out to fleece 'ya."

With a wink and a wave, he drove away leaving Cameron staring at a solid, iron studded oak door. Before he could step up and lift the ornate knocker, the door opened and there stood Trisha.

The dark crescents under her eyes told him she hadn't been sleeping well. Their bluish tinge made her face seem paler than he remembered it, but he hadn't forgotten the depth in her lovely green eyes. It wasn't the expression of surprise he saw in them that stunned him, but the toddler slung across her hip. His jaw tightened and he jerked his head in the child's direction.

"Was that something you ever intended telling me about?"

He watched her throat work as she swallowed and although she opened her mouth a couple of times it was several moments before any sound emerged.

"He's not—"

"Hers, he's mine," chirped in another girl as she emerged from behind the door. She plucked the little boy from Trisha's hip while she looked Cameron up and down. "His name is Sam, I'm Camille Langdon and you're gorgeous. God, Patti, if you don't snap him up I will."

"You can't, you're already married," Trisha mumbled. She still hadn't taken her eyes off Cameron.

A chocolate brown Labrador bolted from the interior of the house and squirmed in front him, shining dark eyes pleading for attention.

"Who let the damn dog out?" yelled an unseen male. "She's in heat, blast it."

"Don't worry, I'll get her." Another figure came out from the doorway, an older woman this time and surely Trisha's mother from the similarity he saw between them. She had a leash in her hand and quickly captured the dog. Cameron stepped back, trying to catch his breath and sort out who was who in this chaotic pack of people.

At last Trisha, or Patti, he wasn't sure what to call her, took pity on him. A shy smile played over her lips and she came towards him.

"I can explain," he said quietly. His heart bumped painfully under his ribs.

"I'm sure you can," she replied. She stood in front him now, a hint of amusement glinting in her green eyes. "But first I think you should kiss me."

"Here?" Cameron almost choked as he cast a glance at the women standing behind her.

"Here," she insisted and added in a wickedly sexy whisper, "if you love me."

For a moment Cameron didn't think he could have heard her correctly. Love her? Lord help him that was all he wanted to do. He placed his hands on her waist and drew her to him. His mouth dried at the thought of the soft curves beneath the 'I-Love-My-Thoroughbred' logo on her stained white tee-shirt. He slipped one hand behind her back and spread his fingers across her spine. Her leg settled against his as she nestled closer to him.

"I can't believe I'm doing this in front of your mother," he whispered as he leaned in and kissed her.

She tasted as sweet as he remembered and when her arms reached up and around his neck he wrapped his arms around her and held her tight. If this was a dream, he didn't want to wake up. She broke the kiss with a smile on her lips murmuring something about introductions.

His dreamlike state remained as he shook hands with her mother, Susan; took more teasing from Camille Langdon and exchanged a sticky high five with Sam. Finally he came face to face with Trisha's father Jeffrey. Tall and slim with tousled dark hair showing a hint of silver at the temples, he had the look of a much younger man but the calculating expression in his eyes as his glance slid over Cameron indicated a world of maturity.

"So you're the cause of my daughter arriving home looking like a train wreck," he said as he held out his hand.

Cameron felt the blush start on his neck as he shook hands. "That was not my intention, sir."

"Sir?" Jeffrey Somerville raised an eyebrow and grinned. "I like you already. Come on in."

Later, when he'd been allocated a guest room and provided with a pile of fluffy towels worthy of a five-star hotel, Cameron remembered to call his cab driver.

"I'm staying here a few days from the look of it," he said into the phone.

"Okay, guv. Best of luck to you and," a throaty chuckle filtered into Cameron's ear, "I 'ope the lady's worth it."

Cameron didn't waste time on wondering how the driver had known, but he had to say the lady certainly was worth it. He'd hardly been able to take his eyes off her all through dinner when more people appeared to take their places at the table.

With himself, Trisha and her parents, Camille, her husband Martin and son, Sam, there were in addition five more guests. Trisha introduced them all but he immediately forgot their names. What he didn't forget was the fact that they were all here in residence to train with Jeffrey Somerville.

He'd been shown the barns and stabling area, the indoor and outdoor riding arenas, a media room where students studied video recordings of themselves and others. He'd seen the impressive website that Trisha had built advertising her father's talents and the horses they had for sale. Susan Somerville had been delighted to show off her two thoroughbred stallions and Delacourt's dam, the grey mare Delia's Delight, reminded him of his own Rosie. As he toured the property with Trisha's father he made mental notes on how to improve his own business.

When the table had been cleared and the guests dispersed, Cameron found himself at last alone with Trisha.

"Let's go for a walk," she suggested as she took hold of his hand.

"Walk?" He couldn't keep the incredulous tone out of his voice.

"Sweetheart, you're in England now. It's what we do." Trisha laughed at him but it was an easy, loving laugh that wrapped around his heart and warmed his soul.

They left the house and grounds and Trisha took him into the fields surrounding it, pointing out parts of the cross-country course her father had designed and constructed and what difficulties each element presented. They walked along ancient cattle paths below the lip of the hill until they came to a point where he could see, between the slopes of the darkening hills, the shimmer of water in the distance.

"That's the River Severn," Trisha said. "It flows out into the Bristol Channel and then the Irish Sea. That's South Wales beyond the river and—"

He stopped her with a kiss, claiming her mouth before she could catch her breath. She melted in to him and still kissing her, he tumbled her gently back into the grass. He pushed her hair back from her face and gently traced the line of her scar. She didn't stop him.

"Do you know how much I love you?" He kissed her neck.

"Maybe as much as I love you." She shivered as his breath feathered across the sensitive skin of her throat.

He slipped his hand under the hem of her tee-shirt, but she caught it and held it close against her skin.

"You were going to explain something to me," she reminded him as she scooted up into a sitting position and wrapped her arms around her legs.

"Having met your folks and seen your home, I think you've some explaining of your own to do. Trisha Watts, photographer, didn't tell me half of it." He hauled himself up beside her and hugged her.

She laid her head against his shoulder with a sigh and opened her heart to him. He'd seen her interview so already knew much of what she shared with him, but when she recalled the day she crashed, he felt her shudder and tightened his arm around her shoulders.

When she fell silent Cameron kissed her temple. "There's only one thing I'm still curious about, sweetheart."

She looked up at him, a frown creasing her face. "What's that?"

"Who's Tony and is he someone I should worry about?"

"How did you know about Tony?"

Dusk had crept up around them but there was still enough light for him to see the look of puzzlement on her face.

"You called out his name several times in your sleep when you were at my place."

Trisha sighed. "He was nearly my fiancé. He'd asked me to marry him and we were going to buy the engagement ring after the European Championships. Camille had heard rumors that he'd been seen on different occasions with other girls and I didn't believe her. But at about the time I blacked out he was discovered in the back of a horse trailer with a hot-to-trot groom. Then I couldn't ignore the rumors anymore. When he came to see me in hospital after I'd recovered consciousness, I threw him and his flowers out. His cheating was such a betrayal after everything I'd gone through and still had to deal with so no, you don't have to worry about him."

Cameron got to his feet and pulled her up with him. "You do know, don't you, that it's going to be agony sleeping under the same roof as you and not have you in my bed?"

She grinned up at him. "Mack said you were like a bear with a sore head without me."

"You've talked to Mack? What's been going on behind my back woman?"

Trisha threw her arms around him, the laughter bubbling out of her. "When you didn't get in touch with Samantha like we thought you might, he went instead. She phoned me to make sure I wouldn't be mad if she gave Mack my number. Even after he explained everything to me I wasn't sure how I could make it right with you but I never expected you'd arrive right here on my doorstep."

"Sweetheart, I couldn't stay away." Cameron stopped to kiss her. "Did he tell you he's getting married?"

She nodded. "Yep. To Tova. Blonde hair, long legs and pink cowboy boots."

"He wants for them to get married at the ranch." Cameron swallowed. He'd hesitated long enough. He'd known how right she was for him from the moment he touched her but still he hesitated. He had a home, a business. But he needed a wife, someone beside him who would make it all worthwhile. He needed Trisha. "I'd like it to be a double wedding so will you please marry me?"

Her kiss swept away any doubt as to her answer and when he broke away to look into her eyes he saw tears shimmering there. He swept them gently away with his forefinger.

"Just promise me one thing," he whispered.

She looked up at him cautiously. "What's that?"

"Please never, ever, wear pink cowboy boots."

Her whoop of laughter floated away into the night as they walked back to her home. They stopped under the portico and Trisha reached up to pull his head down and kiss him again but the door opened and her father stepped out.

"Patricia Somerville, put that cowboy down." His demand was softened by the underlying bubble of amusement in his voice.

"Sorry, Dad, I can't do that," Trisha said with a grin. With shining eyes she looked up at

Cameron and whispered to him, "Because I'll never stop loving that cowboy."

The End

Other titles by Victoria Chatham from Books We Love

His Dark Enchantress
Cold Gold
On Borrowed Time
Shell Shocked
The Buxton Chronicles Boxed Set

About the Author

The date on Victoria Chatham's driver's licence says one thing but this young-at-heart grandma says another. She will read anything that catches her interest but especially historical and western romance. She loves all four-legged critters, particularly dogs but is being converted into a cat lover by Onyx, an all black mostly Manx cat who helps her write. However, it's her passion for horses that gets her away from her computer to trail ride and volunteer at Spruce Meadows, a world class equestrian centre near Calgary, Alberta, where she currently lives.

She loves to travel and spends as much time as she can with her family in England. Find out more about her and her books at http://bookswelove.net/authors/chatham-victoria/.

Books We Love Ltd.